5

# ICE: DEVIL'S NIGHTMARE MC

LENA BOURNE

# PROLOGUE

Ice

You can take an animal out of the cage, but does that make it free? Not to this animal.

You can give a man the chance to take his revenge, but will that make a difference? Not for this man.

By the time Devil's Nightmare MC freed me from the fighting cage, revenge was the only thing I still dreamed of, the only thing I still wanted. Revenge on Satan's Spawn MC for killing my family and destroying my club.

While their president, Lizard, made me fight in the cage like some dog he reared just for that purpose, the only thing I had the entire time I was the Spawns' prisoner, was my hate, my burning wish to get my revenge. I was alive, but I stopped living long before I got my freedom back. Hate was the only thing that kept me going.

For six years I fell asleep with the fantasy of killing Lizard slowly the last thing on my mind. And the first when I woke up. That's all I thought about during the day too. I lost count of how many men's faces I turned into a bloody broken mess in the cage imagining it was his.

Now I finally got my revenge exactly how I dreamed about getting it.

And now I have nothing. No dreams, no fantasies and no reason for existing anymore.

There's no road that can take me back to the man I was.

ICE

ABOUT FIFTY MILES from my hometown, even the air whooshing past my face started smelling familiar. Trees and grass and earth and a clean wind blowing in from the mountains, it's not just any particular smell, but all of them combined, and they're all exactly the same as what I smelled every time I returned home from a ride. Rain started coming down hard when I was twenty miles out, but it didn't wash the smells away. It's been seven years since I've been here. Seven years since I rode down Lizard and the other Spawns that killed my father and burned down his house. Apart from the familiar smell, this is nothing like a coming home should be.

It started raining that night too, soon after I saved my sister Roxie from Lizard, giving up my freedom in exchange for hers. No. Sacrificing my freedom for my life and hers. Only one of us got to live that life, and it wasn't me. I held onto the hope of one day getting my life back for a year, maybe two, of my captivity. But I lost it well and good after that. Even now that I'm free, I don't have hope that I'll ever have an actual life again.

I doubt this homecoming will change any of that. Just as killing Lizard and the rest of the scum that kept me locked up and made me fight in a cage like some dog, didn't change it. If anything was gonna change it, that was it. But it didn't. It just made me more of an animal. A soulless animal.

I wasn't gonna ride in on the same road I left my hometown on, but I changed my mind at the last moment and circled back. It stopped raining while I did that, and the trees Roxie escaped into are glistening now from the downpour, the raindrops still clinging to the branches and reflecting the grey sky that's gonna send down more rain any minute. I couldn't follow her into the trees that night. And I couldn't die either. So I let Lizard take me. It was a coward's mistake. I should've fought them to the death. I lost my life that night anyway. And everyday I still live is a very cutting reminder of that fact.

I feel nothing as I stop at the turn of the road where I forced Lizard to let Roxie go. The wind's grown cold and still brings drops of rain, the grass in the large field bordering the road is bright green and swaying, and I can smell the mud left by the rain underneath it. I smelled it on that night too, while I knelt on the pavement with a gun to my head, deciding to give up my freedom for my life. I smelled it many times before that night, while I rode on these roads that surround my hometown, as free as any bird. I don't feel any desire to get that back. The only thing I feel is the burning need to kill Lizard and those other Satan's Spawn MC bastards all over again. But they're all dead, so I'm never gonna get the chance to. And that's a problem.

The town is quiet and empty when I reach it, just as it always was on rainy afternoons. Not much to do in the town of White Falls, Illinois, never was and probably never will be. One of the best things about this town was leaving it. I did a lot of that. But I always came back, always rode in through Main Street, just as I did now.

Joe's Hardware Store is still on the corner, still closed for lunch until four PM like it always was. Starburst Diner is still open, it seems, going by its flashing sign, which rises above the first row of buildings that line Main Street. But the mom and pop grocery store run by Ruth and Benny is gone, replaced by a flashy looking modern supermarket. In fact, everything lining main street is flashy and modern, even the cars parked on it.

I do feel something as I leave the town behind and head for my father's home. A tightness in my stomach. It's made up of guilt and regret and wishing things didn't turn out the way they did. That tightness was my constant companion, while I was locked up, always lying just beneath the rage and dreams of revenge. I've lived those dreams now, so the regret is all there is these days. And it's strong enough to make me sick the nearer I get to the burned down ruins of my childhood home.

My father's house was squeezed between the woods and a hill on one side and old, abandoned train tracks on the other. They were like that as far back as I can remember and the road leading out of town runs along them. All that's left of my father's house is the concrete slab overgrown with wild grass, and there's a tree growing out of a crack in it. Bright orange flames had already engulfed the entire house by the time I reached it that night, the air hot and unbreathable, smelling of gasoline. But the rain and snow of the last seven years washed any other evidence of that night away.

The night that ended my life. And my father's. And all my MC brothers'. And my sister's too, I believed for a long time. Looking at all this now, it's like none of that ever happened. Except in my nightmares, there it still happens almost every night.

"I wish I'd come back sooner, Pop," I say into the silence, which is absolute after the echoes of my bike's engine die down. It's still like that once my words fade on the wind.

I was on my way out of town that night, taking one of my many trips out into the unknown, like I liked to do. But I got a frantic, hurried phone call from one of the brothers not long into my ride, telling me the Spawns attacked and to get back. I turned around, but I was too late to prevent anything. Except...

"Roxie got away, Pop," I say into the wind. "She made a good life for herself."

The silence returns.

Lizard had just taken over Satan's Spawn MC a couple of months before they attacked us, and it was no secret that him and my father, the President of Wolves of Hell MC never saw eye to eye. My father wasn't overly worried about it though, didn't think

Lizard's hatred would lead to anything. Especially not what it led to in the end.

Everything was already burning when I returned that night—the clubhouse, most of the member's houses and this house too. Everyone was dead or dying, including my father, including the wives and the girlfriends, even some of the club whores. I was too late to save any of them, and I wanted to die with them.

"But I chickened out at the last minute, didn't I, Pop?"

The world stays as silent as it does every time I speak to him like this. I doubt my father can hear me, wherever he is.

"I wish I'd stayed home that night," I say anyway. But I told him all this before, over and over again.

"At least, Roxie lived, that's something, right?"

More silence. About a year into my imprisonment, Lizard lied to me that he tracked her down and destroyed her—even showed me pictures of the bloodied and mutilated corpse of a black haired girl. That killed the last shred of my hope. I'm happy it turned out to be a lie. But not as happy as I should be, not in my heart as any normal man would be.

"Lizard got his," I add and wish I could kill him all over again.

More silence follows. This time I don't break it by speaking like a madman to the wind.

My father's been dead for seven years. None of this matters to him anymore. And if there is a Hell, he already met Lizard and the rest of those Spawns scumbags there.

I try to think of other things, try to remember the way it used to be when our house still stood here. But it's no use. Too much time has passed, and too many other memories are filling my brain between then and now. I don't remember this place as my home. I just remember it as something I lost. Something that can never be replaced. And all I feel is hatred and rage. It wasn't even a mistake coming here. It was just pointless.

There's no life for me anywhere. I lost it on my knees in the rain the night everyone I cared for died. Everyone except Roxie, but she was dead to me for so long, it stirs nothing inside me knowing I was wrong about that.

There's no peace for me anywhere either. I thought I might find it here, by returning full circle back to the place where it all ended. I was wrong. All I have is my freedom, for what that's worth.

ROXIE WANTED me to visit Pop's grave and put some flowers on it, which I find totally pointless, since what the fuck good are flowers anyway? But she'd probably know if I lied to her about doing it, so I did it.

What I meant to do was bury the knife I used to kill Lizard and most of the top ranking members of his club next to my father's tombstone, a symbolic gesture to show him he's been avenged, and to give him the tool I used to do it. But when it came to it, I didn't wanna part with the knife. I like looking at it, I like carrying it on my belt, and I like taking it out from time to time to remember what I used it for. It gives me the little peace I can still find.

Realizing that didn't help my already sour mood any, and I didn't stick around at the communal burial plot where they laid him to rest, because there was no one around to bury him proper. I should be buried right beside him. And I couldn't stop wishing it were true all the while I was there, so I left in a hurry.

Hawk, Devil's Nightmare MC info-gatherer found the gravesite for me. He also found the last remaining Wolves of Hell MC member still living—Denco. He was burned bad and shot, but he lived. Denco was my father's enforcer and close friend besides, but he's at least seventy years old now and by the looks of things, he's about as far removed from MC life as anyone can get.

It's raining hard again, and I've been sitting on my bike in the trees near his hilltop cabin for a couple of hours now, deciding whether to go and knock on his door or leave him be. He's another person who deserves to hear that the Spawns are all gone, that they paid for what they did to us. But he seems to have found his peace and maybe I shouldn't mess that up by stirring memories. And seeing someone who survived, someone who remembers, will just make my black mood worse. Roxie's different, she's my sister, but Denco, he's a brother in arms. Someone who might not understand how I could work for the enemy for so long, because I was too much of a chicken shit to lay down my life for the club.

I almost turned my bike around and rode back down the hill and back into oblivion a couple of times while I sat here. But once the rain lets up at twilight I find myself walking through the tall grass surrounding his mountain cabin. He should die knowing the full story. I think he'd appreciate it.

The light in the cabin turned on as night fell. He's home. And that's all the thinking I do before I knock on the door.

He opens it wide immediately, pointing a sawed-off shotgun at my chest, and squinting with his one good eye. Half his face is burned right off, and the ends of his fingers are missing on both his hands, but he's gripping that shot gun just fine.

"What's your business here?" he barks. "I've been watching you out there in the trees all afternoon."

I put my hands up like I'm surrendering to him. "It's me. Ice. I didn't mean to frighten you."

He squints at me even harder, leaning forward to get a better look. The shotgun drops in his hands as he recognizes me.

"By God, so it is," he says with an air of total surprise and shock. "I heard rumors you were alive, but I dismissed them as bullshit."

It's impossible to tell if he's happy to see me or what, but he did lower the shotgun all the way.

"Not bullshit," I say and chuckle. "And Lizard and the rest of his MC got theirs now. I thought you should know that."

"I heard rumors about that too," he says and opens the door all the way. "Come on in. Maybe you can help me sort out the bullshit from the facts."

I follow him into the cabin, the wooden floor-boards creaking under my boots just like they did that night we cornered five Spawns in a cabin a lot like this one. The boards didn't creak anymore by the time we left, because they were soaked in blood.

I don't know how much of that I'm gonna tell the old guy though. I became a different person during those killings, had trouble reining myself in even when I tried. The monster inside me, which made me the undefeated Death Match champion for six years running, became much more blood thirsty after I was freed, and it's still thirsty. Some of the Devil's Nightmare MC members called me Ice the Butcher behind my back, and if the killings went on much longer, they'd probably start calling me that to my face. I'm not sure I'd mind.

"Sit," Denco instructs me once we reach the kitchen. I do it while he pulls a label-less bottle filled with a golden brown liquid from a cupboard. He sets it and two glasses down in front of me.

I doubt he's washed those glasses any time in the recent past, but I don't comment on it as he pours. It was pointless worrying over it anyway, since the liquor burns my throat like fire, meaning it's probably strong enough to kill any and all germs.

"So, what happened to you?" Denco asks after he empties his own glass. "I heard you fought for Lizard in his tournaments. Heard you were his pride and joy for a long time."

I don't like the edgy light in his eyes or the accusation in his tone. I don't like it one bit. But I know Lizard liked to spread that lie around, and I understand how it must've sounded to Denco, the sole survivor of Wolves of Hell MC. And I agree that letting Lizard keep me prisoner was wrong.

"He kept me locked up like some fighting dog and only let me out when it was time to fight," I say and reach for the bottle to pour myself some more of the drink. Not like it's gonna help any, but it won't hurt either. "But, yeah, I should've let him send me to Hell and I should've taken him with me, instead of letting him keep me locked up."

Denco doesn't say anything, and if it weren't for the sound of his raspy, old man breathing filling the room, I'd swear I was alone. That's how I am most of the time anyway. Alone in my head. Just like I was for the six years Lizard kept me under lock and key. I didn't even speak much for most of those years.

"I'm glad you stayed alive, son," Denco finally says. "All we got is this one life and no guarantees of anything better after it ends. I hate to speak ill of the dead, but your daddy underestimated Lizard and we all paid the price."

"Lizard paid his price too," I say darkly, the night it happened clear before my eyes like it's unfolding at this very moment. "He died choking on his own blood while trying to hold in his guts and keep them from spilling out all over the place. I delivered the bill and collected the payment myself."

The satisfaction I got from killing Lizard was dark, but it was the closest to joy I've felt in a very long time. It didn't bring me relief. Or peace. It was a thing that needed doing, and I did it. But it didn't make anything right again.

"The rest of Satan's Spawns MC followed him to Hell soon after," I conclude. "The ones I killed died in pain and fear. The Wolves of Hell MC has been avenged."

"Good," Denco says and it sounds like he's speaking through gritted teeth. "Wolfman would be proud."

I imagine my father *would* be proud, I just don't know what he'd make of the man I became. But I'll never know, so it hardly matters.

"Ain't nothing gonna bring any of them back," Denco says while pouring himself another shot of his moonshine poison. "That's what rankles the most about this whole thing. My wife and my son were killed. Your sister too, poor girl. And all the brothers. I should've died too."

"My sister's alive," I say. "Lizard took her, but she escaped when they captured me, and she has a good life out West now."

Denco's face brightens at the news, the change clearly noticeable even in the dim light.

"Now, that's some good news," he says and pours

me more of the moonshine liquor. "We gotta toast that."

We do, and we drink, but then there's nothing left to say. The room is filled with ghosts from our past now, at least it seems that way to me, and they're loud, too loud to ignore.

"What are you gonna do now?" Denco asks.

"I don't know yet," I answer truthfully.

Roxie desperately wants me to be a part of her life, but I won't join Devil's Nightmare MC. I'll never call anyone brother ever again. I've mourned too many brothers already.

"Be careful around here," Denco warns. "The Kings and the Bloods are still dividing up the Spawns' leftovers, and it's messy. Most of them won't be too happy to hear you helped dispatch the Spawns either. They let me live as a living reminder of what happens to those that crossed them, but I doubt you'll get a very warm welcome from any of them."

"Don't worry about me. I'm not staying," I say and stand up, because the ghosts are screaming in my ears now, and I can't stay here a minute longer.

"I'm glad you came to see me," Denco says and stands up too. "Good luck, son."

I take the hand he's offering and shake it, but don't say anything.

There's nothing left to say.

I'll find the nearest bar and continue drinking there. Maybe one of the Kings or one of the Bloods will even come to me looking for an argument and a fight. I'll gladly oblige too. The raging monster inside me needs to be fed, it's been starving for too long. And a good fight is probably the only thing that'll silence the ghosts tonight.

2

BARBIE

"WHAT? YOU'RE STILL SLEEPING?" Brick yells while kicking the mattress hard.

*I was until a second ago.* I don't say that, just think it, because I know better.

"It's almost two PM," he barks as he throws the blackout curtain on the window open, ripping it off the hangers by the sound of it.

"You look like shit," he complains, glaring at me as I sit up in bed.

I rub my eyes, wincing as I do, because my fingers caught on the black eye he gave me last night. That's probably what he's referring to. But I don't remind him of that either, because I know better.

"Be at Boar's Pit Stop by nine, and you better look your best," he says harshly.

"OK, Brick, I'll be there," I tell him after a pause, since he's waiting for me to speak. I hoped I'd get the night to myself tonight.

He really had a go at me last night, mostly because he couldn't keep his dick hard. My head still hurts from the punch that left me with the bruise. Everything hurts, and on top of it, I couldn't get to sleep until past dawn worrying about it all.

"You better," he spits, tosses a couple of twenty-dollar bills on the foot of the bed, and strides out the room. A few moments later I hear the front door slam shut.

I've been Brick's woman, since I was twenty-five years old, and I'm almost thirty now. He's never gonna make me his old lady. I'm just plain getting too old for him. Worrying about that is what kept me up all night, while he snored beside me and my head throbbed.

Brick's never been a gentle guy, but he's gotten even rougher these past few months. I think it's because he's sick of me. But where the hell am I gonna go if he dumps me? I have no money except what he gives me, and no skills to make it either.

And I'm almost thirty years old and look it. Over the hill. No prospects and no way out of this life I entered so happily and joyously at seventeen. The fucking idiot that I was. And still am.

Boyfriends were easy to come by when I was younger and prettier. There was always a new one just around the corner when an old one kicked me to the curb. But I should've found an old man by now. That was the plan. Yet all I got for my efforts was a string of losers slapping me around until I landed with Brick. He was older and a president of his club, Kings of the Road MC, and I thought I had it made when he chose me. But he's proven to be the worst of them all.

Love, I thought it was at the beginning, but I grew out of that delusion right quick after the third time he beat me bloody. But by then he'd never let me go. He's one of those who consider a woman their property. I could try to run, but I'd probably not get very far. And what would I do? I can't even strip for Christ's sake.

"Stop feeling sorry for yourself, Barbie," I tell myself out loud, and refuse to think about any of that anymore while I take my shower.

I succeed, for the most part, until I finally get a good look at my face in the mirror and realize that I do in fact look like shit, because the bruise around my eye is covering half my cheek as well. And I'm fresh out of the good foundation that covers it all.

"Fuck my life!" I yell and fling the empty bottle against the mirror, wasting what little was left of the foundation and making a mess.

But I didn't get this far in life by not doing what needed to be done. And I could use a walk to clear my head and to get out of this house that's more or less my prison, and a lasting reminder of the mess that is my life.

So I scrape the foundation off the mirror, use it to cover my black eye as best I can, put on a hoodie, a baseball hat and the biggest pair of sunglasses I own, pocket the money Brick gave me and head for the mall. At least he's generous with the cash he gives me, some girls don't even have that luxury.

I'll get the prettiest dress I can afford at the mall, and all the makeup I need. Maybe, just maybe, I'm wrong. Maybe Brick means to keep me around. Maybe it's just the stress with the MC that has him all riled up. He's fighting with the Bloods over dividing what's left of the Spawns' operation. Of course his nerves are frayed.

It's the same lie I've been telling myself for the better part of the year, but it still sorta makes me feel better.

THE MALL IS CROWDED like it always is on rainy days. And it's coming down in buckets outside now. I narrowly escaped getting drenched on my way here, but it doesn't look like I'll be so lucky on the way back.

I've already bought all I needed to buy, including a very nice new dress - red, because that's Brick's favorite color, and short, because he likes that too. I also got all the makeup I needed, and applied some right away in the bathroom, since I looked ridiculous walking here with my high-summer sunglasses on, and I looked even more ridiculous wearing them indoors. Plus, I couldn't see anything with them on, since the lenses are completely black.

I've just been browsing around the huge, two-floor beauty shop for the past hour or so, getting trailed by employees, since I look like the type that's gonna steal. I'm not gonna steal, because I'm not a thief and never was. So if they have the time, let them watch me. It's their loss. I bet some of these prim and proper girls shopping today are stealing, but no, they're gonna go with the obvious choice. The white trash girl. The biker slut. They could be serving people, but instead they wanna make me feel bad with their accusatory looks and not a shadow of a smile when they ask me if I need some assistance. I don't need their assistance. I know how to make myself look gorgeous. The assistants do smile a lot at the other girls and women in here, and for some reason that's making me feel really low today. Probably because I haven't been smiled at in a very long time. But I don't want to think about that.

"Excuse me," one of the shopping women says, but doesn't wait for me to get out of the way from where I've been crouching to check out the blushes, and nearly knocks me over.

She doesn't even glance at me, let alone apologize. She's one of those privileged, polished pretty girls that no store clerk would ever assume is gonna steal. Long and perfectly straightened brown hair with highlights are spilling down to the middle of her back, she's wearing an outfit straight from the latest fashion spread, and her nails are done to a T. I bet her manicures last for a week or more, unlike mine, because I'm always chipping and breaking my nails on something. I wish I could grow my hair out past my shoulders, but it just gets all thinned out and scraggly looking once it reaches that point. It's from all the peroxide I've been torturing it with, because I like being a blonde, and Brick likes it that way too. Or maybe he doesn't care, and I just like to pretend

I'm doing things to please him when in fact I can't. Not anymore.

I bet this woman's boyfriend doesn't beat her. I bet he treats her well, like an equal. Maybe he's even one of the bored looking dudes standing by the door and playing with their phones, while clutching shopping bags bulging with the stuff their wives or girlfriends already bought. I think I'd like a guy who'd do that for me, but none of the ones I've dated so far would set foot in a mall even when I asked them to.

"Can I help you with something?" the woman asks sternly, making me realize I've been staring at her while all of that shot through my brain.

"No, I'm good," I tell her and walk away.

I bet she has a doormat of a men at home to order around, going by that perfectly clipped and bossy tone she just used with me, which can only get that perfect with practice. Who wants that kinda guy? That's not a man at all, just a manly woman.

I leave the store, would leave the mall altogether, since I don't really belong in this world of high maintenance, normal women and their doormat men, and I never did. But it's still raining buckets outside.

And the longer I sit on the bench by one of the large windows overlooking the parking lot, and the shabby part of town where I live beyond it, the more

I wish I'd never come here. I'm getting that empty feeling in the pit of my stomach that I always get when I acknowledge just how much is missing from my life, and how I'll never be able to fill it, because I'm too old, too used up, too spent and not good at anything but being some guy's good time girl. I'm not even steady girlfriend material, let alone wife. I'm just a booty call.

And the sight of all these normal couples, guys and girls my age, roaming around the mall holding hands is making it worse. It's not a painful emptiness. It's just sad. And when the sadness tips over and overflows, it's hard to claw my way back out and accept my life for what it is — as in, not as bad as it could be.

Plenty of women everywhere have it worse than me. Plenty of them are stuck in dead-end, abusive relationships, with as little chance and skill to get out as me.

Most times when I get like this, it makes me feel better to know that. But today it's not working. I blame the rain and not getting enough sleep, and the fact that my head is still pounding.

Damn it, just once I'd like to have a guy look at me with more than just lust, or kiss me because he loves me, not because he just wants to fuck me, or hold the door open for me, or hold his jacket over my head, so I don't get wet as we run to get to our car in the parking lot, or value my opinion and take my feelings into account. Someone who loves me with all his heart and gives me all his devotion.

I never had any illusions that I'd amount to much in life, not with how partying and being wild and free was always my top priority, but damn it, I was sure I'd find a guy like that for myself. Someone I'll love just as much as he loves me and just as deeply.

But clearly, I was wrong.

I won't dwell on it anymore, because it's pointless. There aren't enough pieces of my heart left to fall in love with anyone new. I've used them all up, wasted and squandered away all the love I had to give on the wrong guys and now it's all gone. I settled for Brick and I'm gonna keep him.

So I grab my shopping bags and head out into the rain. I'll get my hair done, I'll get my nails done, and I'll wear my gorgeous new dress tonight. And then none of these normal women who got what they wanted will be able to hold a candle to me. Because I'm sure almost none of them have enjoyed themselves half as much as I've enjoyed my life so far. Or been as free and wild.

So what if I'm getting older? MILFs are a hot commodity nowadays. It'd help if I had an actual child to go with it, but Brick saw to it that I'll never get pregnant again when he beat my baby out of me. A two percent chance of ever getting pregnant again is what the doctor said afterwards. Which is just doctor speak for *when pigs fly*.

And there I go again, thinking about the bad.

I just have to not think of the bad and then everything's good. It's as good a strategy for coping with life as any. Because the most important thing is to keep moving forward, in whatever way you can.

# 3

ICE

I should've picked a different bar to drink at. This one reminds me too much of what should've been. And what was. But Boar's Pit Stop was always the one place where it didn't matter where you came from or where you were going or what club you belonged to. Old Boar made sure of that. He came to this country after the big war in Europe, an Englishman who fell in love with an American nurse so he followed her here. He never belonged to any MC, but he liked to ride, so he wanted to build a place where all outsiders would be welcome. I'm an outsider in my own hometown now, so it seemed fitting I come here to drink.

Boar's long gone now, and was already long gone before I disappeared. But I remember when that Boar's head hanging over the bar always looked spiffy and new because he cleaned it once a month. I remember coming here with my father when I was a kid and watching him do it. He'd tell me stories about how he caught that boar himself, in the woods around this town, but that was probably a lie since the story kept changing each time he told it. Now it looks ratty and ready to be thrown out. It also doesn't look like everyone's welcome here anymore.

In the two hours I've been here, four fights broke out, one of which might prove fatal to the guy who got his head smashed in. They just dragged him out the back door and probably left him there. The only club colors I'm seeing are those belonging to the Blood Riders MC and Kings of the Road MC, which were both very small outfits back when my father ran things around here, but they seemed to have moved up in the world.

I've been getting a lot of looks, most of them followed by loudly whispered conversations that I know are about me without needing to hear the words. I'm a fucking legend as far as anyone who followed Death Match is concerned, and that's most bikers from here to Cali and back again. I'm the undefeated champion for six years running. For life, now that I'm no longer fighting. That's also pretty much all I've got to show for my life, but it's something, when you look at it that way. And hell, maybe after a couple more drinks, I'll give some of these whispering fuckers the chance to try and take the title away from me. They won't.

But for now I'm happy just watching the blonde in the red dress.

She came in about half an hour ago, sauntered right up to the bar and ordered a glass of wine. Until that moment, I didn't even know they served wine at this place.

She looks like one of those pinup girls old-timers liked to put on their biceps, complete with her hair done up just so, a bright red dress and nails and lips to match. She's curvy but not overly so, and her smooth, milk white legs go on forever. In other words, she's exactly my type.

She makes all the other ladies in here fade into the background, and she kinda glows like there's an invisible spotlight floating just above her head. I wouldn't mind taking her with me when I leave this place. It's been awhile since I fucked a woman. And it's been even longer, since I wanted to as much as I want to fuck this one. I bet those long legs of hers would feel real nice wrapped around my hips. Or spread wide open. That'd be a sight too. I bet she can take it. And if her coy glances my way are anything to go by she likes to take it too.

She's gorgeous, but all the other guys in here are ignoring her. And that could only mean one thing. She belongs to someone none of these guys want to fuck with. I have no such niceties to observe. I'm a ghost around these parts. I could go over there and talk to her, and I'll do just that if her man doesn't show up in the next five minutes. Fuck consequences, fuck the fact that the only guy for thousands of miles around here that I could count on to have my back is an old man with half his face burnt off. Fuck all that, I like her smile. And I don't have much to live for.

Used to be I had friends everywhere I turned around here. I got drunk with some of them more than once at this very table. And in the alley behind this bar, where they left that guy who got his head smashed in, that's where I got the best blowjob of my life. From Maxine. She's gone now too.

But I bet the woman in the red dress gives great blowjobs, and I wouldn't mind smearing that bright red lipstick of hers. She's still smiling at me as though she'd like that too. I should go talk to her. Even if she belongs to some hardass that can't stand others even looking at his woman.

What else have I got to lose? I already lost it all. Along with my sanity and my common sense. A good blowjob would go a long way to making me feel better, a good fuck even further. And she looks like a good fuck.

But just as I decide to make my move and stand, the door opens and an old guy with grey in his beard walks in, flanked by a couple burly looking old-timers. I'd pay it no mind and continue on my quest, but the whole room sorta freezes, including the woman in the red dress who's got the brightest smile on her face now, as she looks at him. That smile makes her look younger and much happier than she did before the guy walked in. It's so bright it makes me wish she was smiling at me like that, because it's been a long, long time since any woman did that.

But it's a passing thought. I plop my ass back down and finish off the rest of my Jack, because, yeah, she clearly does belong to someone else, and she obviously likes it just fine that way.

And seeing her wrap her slender arms around his neck once he reaches her chases away the last of my desire to fuck. Or do anything but get so drunk I won't remember anything about this day.

Coming back home was a mistake. There's nothing to find here, unless it's more regret and guilt, and I don't need any more of that.

---

BARBIE

FIGURES BRICK WOULD BE late meeting me. He always is when he tells me to meet him somewhere, it's just one of the ways he likes to show me who's boss. The wait would be a lot more unpleasant if it weren't for the hot stranger sitting alone in the more shadowy part of the bar.

Normally, I'm ignored when I come in here alone, because Brick can't stand other guys being near me unless he gives the OK. That never made a whole lot of sense to me, because he likes watching me getting fucked by other men, it's one of the few things that never fails to get him going lately. But it has to be on his say so, on his terms, everything always does, and his men seem fine with that arrangement. There's no not being fine with it anyway. It's his way or the highway, I learned that lesson the hard way a few times over.

But this new guy doesn't know about Brick's rules. He's been checking me out since I walked in, and he's not growing tired of doing it either. It's been years since a guy kept looking at me with that kind of desire, and it feels good. So good, I even smiled at him a few times, even though that's dangerous since someone could see me do it and tell Brick. But I've been feeling so old and washed out and unwanted lately, and his clear desire makes all that fade like it hasn't in years. As stupid as it sounds, I feel like I'm twenty-one again and every guy's wet dream, just like I used to feel back then. I know it's all in my head, but it feels good, so I'm going with it.

This guy also looks a whole lot better than most of the guys I see around here. That's pure muscle under that leather jacket of his and no sign of a beer belly. And those eyes, man, they're intense enough to pull me right into his lap. They're green, I think, or maybe blue, but definitely not boring old brown.

I'm pretty sure he was about to come over and chat me up right before Brick and his inner circle walked in and rudely interrupted it all. But at least our brief exchange of looks made it much easier to give Brick one of my biggest smiles. The kind that made him choose me as his lady over all others all those years ago. I thought I'd hit it big then, thought I got all I ever wanted, because the president of a club wanted me. The years since showed me different, but I still have it better than a lot of other women, and tonight I'm gonna fight to keep it. The stranger looks good and we'd probably have a good time together. But having a good time is overrated, and it doesn't keep a roof over your head. I learned that lesson pretty well too.

"You kept me waiting," I croon as I wrap my arms around Brick's neck, looking at him like he's the only guy worth looking at in this whole place. "You know I don't like that."

"I was busy," he says and doesn't even crack a smile as he removes my arms from around his neck. I swear I'd have more luck flirting with a wall than I do with him lately, and that realization snaps me right back into the middle of all the worrying that kept me up all night.

"You're not gonna do much waiting on him anymore," Bub, one of his enforcers, says, and chuckles, making the breath I was taking freeze in my throat. He stops chuckling after a sharp look from Brick, which just makes me worry even more.

"What's that supposed to mean?" I ask Brick, demanding an answer too harshly, even though I know he doesn't like that.

"Guess the cat's out of the bag," Brick mutters and turns to Bub. "Might as well go get him. But I wanted to do this in private."

Bub nods curtly and leaves. The other guys Brick brought with him close the gap he left in their ranks as they flank me. They're standing too close, as though they're here to prevent my escape and my heart is racing in my throat now, my breaths all jagged and painful. And the panic just gets worse as Bub returns, because he's trailed by the one guy I always make a point of avoiding, which isn't easy since he makes a point of stalking me. Razor. The president of Blood Riders MC. He was once Brick's sworn enemy, but lately they've become buddies. He's also been obsessed with me, since the first night I wandered into this place looking for a good time.

"What's he doing here?" I ask, not even trying to hide my fear and anger.

"He's here to collect you," Brick says. "I'm glad you dressed up all nice and pretty like I told you to. It'll make him that much happier."

"Collect me like how?" I ask, the room now spinning before my eyes, the air all stuffy like I'm suffocating because they're all standing so close and there's no escape for me. This is worse than my worst nightmare, because I don't think Brick just wants to lend me to Razor for the night so he can watch me get fucked by him. I think he means to give me to him for good.

"It hasn't been working between us for awhile now, baby, you know that," Brick says sweetly enough, but there's such meanness in his eyes I have to look away. "Me and Razor recently struck a deal, and you're the sweetener. He's been lusting after you for years."

Razor is standing next to me now and smiling widely, showing me all his rotted black teeth. He's old, even older than Brick, and looks meaner, much meaner. His smile is stretching his face into a grimace, but his brown eyes are cold like the grave.

"I'm not going with him," I snap. "What the fuck? You can't just give me away. You don't own me."

I try to push my way past the men encircling me, but Brick grabs my arm roughly and pulls me back so hard my spine slams against the edge of the bar counter. And I know then that I have no chance of getting away, but I also know I'm not going down without a fight. I never do.

"You'll do what I tell you to do," Brick barks at me. "And I'll have none of your lip tonight."

He thrusts me at Razor who grips me just as tightly by my other arm, but I shake it off violently.

"Settle down, gorgeous," Razor says. "You'll like where we're going."

"I'm not going anywhere with you!" I yell and try to free myself from his grasp, but his fingers around my arm are like a vise.

"Oh, but you are," he says softly, acting as though I didn't just yell at him.

"Like hell I am, let me go!" I yell, and in a dumbass fit of inspiration like I sometimes get, because I'm an idiot, I follow it up by spitting in his face.

The flash in his eyes is the only warning I get before his fist collides with my cheek, the pain from the bruise already there mixing with the one that'll cause a new one, making me see double before everything goes black. The sharp pain in my wrist as it twists while I try to catch myself to prevent my head from slamming against the bar is the only thing that keeps me from losing consciousness.

I can take a punch, that's something I learned in my life too, something Brick and many of the guys before him taught me, but the room is still mostly black before my eyes, as someone yanks me to my feet.

I didn't pass out from the punch, but it'd probably be better if I had, because this night isn't ending anywhere I want to be. My future doesn't look too good either, for that matter, if Razor wasted no time almost knocking me out before he even took me home.

———————

ICE

WELL, she was real happy to see that old man of hers, but she doesn't seem that happy with whatever he came here to tell her. The bar visibly cleared when they started arguing, tough bikers running out like a bunch of hens. There's just me, them and a couple guys too drunk to know where they are left in this place. Even the bartender removed himself to the back room. But I can't hear what they're arguing about since this damn song is too loud.

And that's probably for the best. Whatever's going on is none of my business. The sum total of my plan for tonight was to get blackout drunk, crash somewhere for the night, and then leave this town behind, never to return.

But as it is, I'm only just drunk enough to notice the fear and distress in her eyes, and to want to do something about it. But whenever I get this urge to save a woman it never ends well for me. I'm not talking about Roxie, she's my little sister, and I'd lay my life on the line for her anytime. I'd even go through all that shit with Lizard all over again, if it meant she'd be safe and protected. I knew that since the moment she was born, pretty much. But there was also Rook's woman in Mexico and saving her landed me right back in a windowless cell for a spell. I've also gotten into my share of fights for stepping in over ladies getting mistreated. But that was before Lizard and Death Match.

Maybe I should step in now. I've been so fucking nostalgic and depressed lately, and the drink alone ain't helping. I need a good fight, that always helped. Not so much on the mornings after, when there was pain on top of the regret, hate and depression. But if I manage to get her out of here, I'm sure I'll get a couple nights of very good gratitude sex out of her before they track us down.

Yet there's easier ways to find a woman to fuck. This one is well and truly spoken for, and it's not my way to mess with another man's woman.

But her eyes keep growing wider and more fearful, since that other, even older guy came in, and they're very beautiful eyes. She shouldn't be this afraid; she's too pretty for that. And she did make my evening better by letting me look at her and smiling at me. I can take the five old-timers giving her a hard time with my left hand, it's the ones waiting outside we gotta worry about. But fuck it, today's a good day to die. And long overdue besides.

She yells something that I can't make out over the loud music and gets punched in the face for it. And that decides it for me. I can't fucking watch a woman get hit hard like that by a man, it's too wrong. I don't remember walking over to them, but I'm right behind the guy who punched her as he hauls her to her feet. I was sure she passed out from the punch, but her eyes are open. They're glassy, but she looks conscious enough. She's a tough one, probably used to getting punched. That's another thing I hate about guys like these, they like punching their women.

"What's going on here?" I ask, even though I've already seen all I need to see about this scene. But it's as good a place as any to start this conversation.

They all turn to me, including the lady, but I'm not sure she can see me all that clearly, or see anything for that matter. I was right about her eyes though. They're even prettier up close. Turquoise like the Pacific Ocean, or those marbles I used to collect when I was a kid. I always liked this color best.

"None of your fucking business, that's what," the boyfriend snaps, spittle hitting me in the face. "Who are you, anyway?"

He doesn't recognize me, but some of his posse does and the toothless guy to his left is already whispering something in his ear while staring at me.

His eyes are sizing me up, mockery clear behind the meanness. "Iceman? Is that really you? I've been wanting words with you and that Devil's Nightmare scum over what you did to the Spawns. And now here you are?"

"It's just Ice now." I always hated that nickname Lizard created for me after he took me prisoner. It was a play on my father's name - Wolfman – and a way for him to tell everyone who I was without telling anyone straight out. With me not able to tell my side of the story, a whole bunch of men believed him when he lied that I'd betrayed my MC and joined up with the Spawns to kill them all, so I could fight in the tournaments. Some still believe it. But this guy wouldn't be talking trash about Devil's Nightmare MC if any of them were here now, and he can't be sure they're not. That's my ticket out of this.

"Well, Ice," he says slowly, annunciating my name in an exaggerated way. "I suggest you move along now. You're lucky I got other things to deal with."

"Sure, but I'll be taking her with me. You all need some time to cool off. You're in no fit state to be around the lady right now."

For a second there I forgot my reasons for coming over here, while I remembered Lizard too vividly to see anything else. But her eyes are all cleared up now. She sees me and obviously understands what I'm saying too, which I don't think was the case up until now, since she wastes no time moving to stand behind me. Smart lady.

"What the fuck are you doing, Barbie?" her boyfriend yells and makes to grab her, but I grab him around the throat instead, and press my knife against the soft spot under his jaw. I always keep this knife close, but I don't actually remember drawing it just now. I better make this swift if we're gonna get out of here alive.

"We'll be leaving now," I tell the rest of the guys, some of whom have already drawn their guns.

But I doubt they'll make a move since I have their president in such an unfortunate situation. Go for the throat and make it fast, that's what Cross and the rest of the Devils taught me in this last year, while they helped me round up and dispatch the Spawns. They didn't mean "the throat" literally, but that's what I usually went for, and it works right now too. I look at the woman and jerk my head towards the back door. She runs towards it without a split second of hesitation.

"I used this here knife to cut up about half of the

Spawns myself. So the rest of you just hang tight at the bar if you want your President back alive," I tell the old-timers as I back away, dragging the president with me. I'm hoping not many of the guys who left when these ones came in are hanging out by the back door. The front door is probably another matter.

"How far do you think you'll get?" the guy asks. He's trying to be mocking, but I hear fear in his voice too. His guys aren't making a move to stop me either.

"We'll see," I say and chuckle.

I'm not sure how far me and the woman who's following my lead without needing to be prompted will get. But I figure she'll come away with just a couple more bruises if this fails, whereas I'll probably end up dead, and that's an outcome I can live with.

I turn to tell her to get the door, but she's one step ahead of me and already holding it open.

"Don't follow us if you want him to live," I warn the others, though I'm sure they won't heed that. Why would they? It's two MCs against one man at this point.

"Careful," she says, right before I almost trip over that beat up guy they left out here to die.

It's raining hard again outside, which is a plus,

since the parking lot is bound to be deserted. But we still better make this fast.

"That's my bike," I tell her, pointing at the only one visible from the alleyway.

Then I spin the guy I'm holding around. He was about to say something, but I just give him a few fast and hard punches to the face. He never even got to put up his arms before he slammed against the pavement.

Then I'm clutching her hand and running for my bike, puddles splashing under my boots. Another moment later, she's sitting behind me, plastered to my back with her arms digging into my ribs. But she was right to hold on tight, because I plan on going fast. It's weird how she can anticipate my every move like we're a team.

That's just a passing thought, since doubts are creeping in now that we're speeding through the sleeping, rainy town. I just painted a target on my back from not one, but two MCs. I put her in danger, and probably brought some additional shit down on Roxie and Cross, and Devil's Nightmare MC. And for what? Because some guy punched his old lady? For a girl with pretty eyes? Or because I have a death wish I can't control anymore?

It's that last. And I can already hear the roaring of

bikes behind us as they give chase. I'll drop her off in the next town and disappear.

But she does feel damn good wrapped around my back, and she does have a very pretty smile and even prettier eyes. Maybe I'll keep her a little longer. What's the worst that can happen? We're thousands of miles from California and no one messes with Devil's Nightmare MC unless they absolutely have to.

4

---

Barbie

My head is throbbing and spinning and the pain in my wrist gets worse with every mile we cover. But I keep holding on tight to his back, because those bikes chasing us are getting closer.

This stranger who just saved me from my worst nightmare seems to know all the roads around here pretty well. We're rocking down a gravel path that soon disappears in a dense copse of trees, the sound of the bikes after us fading into the distance. The gravel road just keeps going onwards though. I've lived in this town for five years and I never knew there was a road here. I hope Brick and them don't either. Though I don't think Brick will be getting up from that beating anytime soon. Good. It serves him right.

He slows down, guiding his bike off the gravel road and stops behind a thick tree. We're completely out of sight, especially after he kills the lights. But the sky cleared with that last downpour, and the full moon I saw rising as I headed for the bar earlier gives off enough light to see by perfectly.

My wrist is burning in pain as I finally release my hold on his waist. Not that I want to let go of him. For some reason, holding onto him felt so good it trumped the pain in my face, head and wrist, as well as the one caused by the cold rain coming down so hard it damn near broke skin. Our ride to this tree felt like a new beginning, and he felt better, more solid, more present than any other guy I've ever ridden with. And there have been plenty of those in my past. But yeah, that's probably just because I most likely have a concussion and I'm ecstatic that it's not Razor I'm riding with. I don't remember much of what went on after Razor punched me in the bar, just bits and pieces, but I do know this man stepped in to save me.

He looks damn good up close too, I realize as he gets off the bike and we're standing face to face. He's rugged and unshaved, and he must've broken his nose a couple of times in the past, and probably some of the other bones in his face too, since the scars are visible even by moonlight. But there's something else in his face too, something that suggests there's more to his story than just violence and getting drunk and fucking, which is the sum total of the lives of the men I've known. He's tall too, and wide, and hard, and I'm sure the muscles I've been resting against, and which he used to level Brick with the ground with almost no effort, would be a sight to see in the flesh.

"That was a very stupid thing you did back there," I blurt out. Very untactful on my part, and I blame my concussion, but I also know the kinda man Brick is and he will never let this stand. He's gonna be gunning for this stranger's blood now.

"A simple thank you would do," he says, his lips curling up into a lopsided grin and making his face look even more intriguing. "Or are you saying you'd like to go back?"

I shake my head, drops of water from my wet hair flying everywhere. The rain stopped, but we're drenched and water is still dripping off the both of us.

"I never want to go back there." I smile and offer him my hand. "Let me start this over. Thank you for helping me out and getting us out of there,

Ice. I'm Barbie, and no, I don't want to go back there."

I remember him telling Brick and them his name back at the bar. That was the moment I started comprehending the world around me again. The song that was playing while we made our escape is still sounding in my mind. I always loved that song and it was the perfect soundtrack to what was happening.

He takes my hand, firmly but not harshly, and I get an actual electric shock from the touch, it shakes me right to the core. I've heard other women talk about feeling that when they touched a particularly desirable man, and I thought I'd come close to it with other guys, but not like this, it was never this strong. But that's probably just the concussion talking.

"Barbie like the doll?" he asks and laughs like it's the stupidest thing, but he's still holding my hand, which feels nice, so I don't really mind his reaction that much.

"Yeah, that's my name, and I think it's cute," I say rather too defensively, probably. "What does a guy like you know about dolls anyway? You got daughters or something?"

*Oh, smooth, Barbie. You can barely stand and you're already checking if he can be your next man. Why don't you just come out and ask where his wife's at?* She's probably back home where he left her with their kids, while he came out to have some fun.

He grins again. "No daughters, but I had a sister who liked playing with dolls a lot. She tried to get me to play with her, but I draw the line at dolls."

The look on his face tells me he's remembering a treasured memory from his past, but it turns all pained and twisted before he even finishes speaking. He's also let go of my hand, and I kinda miss the warmth of his palm. I have no idea what shifted his mood from playful to this hardness that's on his face and in his stance now. But then again, he did just beat up the president of an outlaw MC and maybe that fact is just dawning on him now.

"I have to sit down," I say and stagger rather than walk to the trunk of the tree.

"Alright, yeah, do that," he says peering at the start of the road we took to get here. "But we ain't staying long. Just long enough to see if they know about this road, and if we have to go deeper into the woods to hide. For the time being, it looks like we got away."

"They'll come looking for us, that's for sure," I say.

I feel very light and warm despite the chill in the air and me being soaking wet and wearing almost nothing. I figure that's a problem, as is the fact that I just want to go to sleep.

"What's the plan now?" I ask, sitting up straight, since I know I shouldn't be falling asleep.

He points off into the trees behind my back somewhere. "We'll follow this road to the next town over. If we're lucky they don't know about this shortcut. After that, it's probably best if we both disappear."

"You got some friends in the area that we can crash with?" I ask, slurring the words something awful, like I'm drunk.

There's that hard, pained expression on his face again. I feel it more than see it, since we're so far apart now. It feels like a wall just erupted around where he's standing.

"No, I have no friends anywhere around here," he says.

"Oh, crap. Well, the guy you beat up has plenty of friends from here to Chicago and he's not gonna stop until he finds us." I spoke before thinking better of it, since having no friends obviously doesn't sit well with him, given the hardness in his voice, and the fact that the wall just got a couple of inches thicker.

I was sure he had some backup nearby before getting into that fight, though I might have guessed he was solo, since his jacket is just plain black leather with no patches, nor any trace of them ever being on there. But, Jesus, who gets into a losing fight over a woman he doesn't even know. It feels nice that he did, but maybe that's just because he's insane. Maybe I'd be better off with Razor.

No, that doesn't sound right. I'd never be better off with Razor.

"You're probably right," he says. "We should get outta here before they find us. Can you stand?"

He offers me his hand and I take it, then I let him pull me to my feet, because I'm not very steady in my body right now.

"You're not looking too well there, Barbie," he observes. "You gonna throw up?"

I shake my head, and he takes off his jacket and places it around my shoulders, which is another kind and considerate gesture I'm not used to anymore. It's been a long time, since I was young and free and guys acted like gentlemen around me. So long, I've stopped thinking about those times. But here's this guy, come out of nowhere to show me all I've been missing these last few years I spent with Brick, in the space of less than an hour. And he beat him up too. That's something I've dreamed about seeing for awhile now.

It's a bumpy ride down the forest dirt road we're

taking, but he's not wearing his jacket now, and I can feel every one of his muscles in his back perfectly through his shirt. It's almost like he's not wearing it at all. And I like it. I like it more than I've ever liked leaning against a guy before. Whatever happens now, I'm just glad I got to feel all this once again tonight. He smells fantastic too, like leather and earth and burning wood, kinda like my home did before Granny got sick and before Mom turned into a junkie whore, and everything got very complicated

I can't stay awake anymore. The rocking, his warm body pressed against mine, the memories of home, and the humming of his bike are making it impossible. And who knows, maybe after I wake up, this dream will still be just as nice.

***

"HEY, BARBIE! WAKE UP!" he says rather loudly, and I don't think it's the first time he's said it. When I open my eyes, a bright light sears me right to the brain. I shut them tight again.

He's standing beside the bike, holding me upright and shaking me, not roughly, but it doesn't feel good either.

"Alright, I'm awake," I say and somehow manage

to get my leg over the seat, but actually standing up is beyond me just yet.

"Where are we?" I ask while he helps me off the bike.

"The hospital," he says.

"What? Why?" I ask and open my eyes, which was a mistake because that bright light is frying my brain again and I'm seeing two of him. The light's coming from the ER entrance.

"That was quite a hit you took, and your wrist is the size of a football," he explains. "Trust me, you need to get seen. I have some experience with getting punched and such."

He said it lightly, but his two faces tell me he doesn't mean it that way at all. I look down at my arm, and realize he's right. I'm seeing two of my left wrist and they're both very swollen and purple-looking.

"They'll think you did this to me if we go in, and they'll call the cops," I say.

Brick never came in with me to the ER when I needed it for precisely that reason. Hell, he wouldn't even take me most of the times I probably needed it.

"Don't worry about it," he says and takes his jacket off me. "I'm not going in with you."

That was spoken more like the type of guy I expected him to be.

"This is where we part ways," he adds.

"What? I thought you were taking me with you," I practically yell, and it doesn't make my headache any better. "When Brick finds me, he'll make me pay."

"No need for him to find you," he says. "Just tell them your boyfriend beat you up and have them take you to some shelter. They have to, by law."

"And how do you know that?" I snap. "Because you just go around rescuing battered women all the time?"

He just chuckles at that, but I wasn't saying it to be funny.

"Why'd you even step in anyway?" I ask.

He shrugs. "Spur of the moment thing. I'm no good at impulse control lately and before you got beat up, I was thinking it'd be fun to get to know you better tonight. It didn't click what a mistake me getting involved was until that old boyfriend of yours was on the ground."

"Right, you stormed in and made a mess of things, but now I'm too much of a hassle to keep around. Sure, I get it," I mutter.

He's looking at me very intently, but I can't meet his eyes. This is nothing like the dream I hoped to wake up into when I fell asleep leaning against his back on the bike. Nothing at all. This is more like a nightmare. Where do hell will I go?

"If he finds you, just talk your way out of it and blame it on me. Say I'm just some crazy motherfucker who dragged you away against your will. No one who's heard of me will doubt it," he says. "At least you got more options now than you did back at the bar. That's something, right?"

He's right, for what it's worth. But I don't say anything. I don't want him to just leave, but how do you convince a stranger to stay, when it makes so much more sense for him to disappear? Brick will want revenge for this. And Brick always gets his revenge. He's known for it.

"And like you already figured out, I have no friends around here," he adds. "I can't keep you safe from his entire MC."

I shrug and nod slowly, which makes my headache even worse. "I don't have any friends around here either. Or anywhere, really."

Then I walk away towards the hospital entrance, because there's nothing more to say. He won't stay and I have no right asking him to. And he's not wrong, I do have more options now and he gave them to me. Not sure what I'll do with them, because they still suck, just not as hard, but it's for the best that I don't spoil all the good stuff he did for me by asking for the impossible.

"You're a fine looking woman though," he yells

after me. "I wish we'd met under better circum-stances."

"Yeah, me too," I yell back, but I don't turn to look at him.

Because fuck it, what's the point of looking back? What was ever the point of that? I'm heading forward. Just like always.

# 5

ICE

THE SKY IS clear and all is as silent as the dead of night always is around these parts. No one followed us here. Guess those old fuckers don't know the back roads around here the way I know them. If I leave now, I'll be long gone by dawn. I should leave. Disappear. Tonight's episode was a mistake, one that's only gonna get compounded, if I keep her around after I already stole her. They'll find her tomorrow, or, what's even more likely, she'll go back to them tomorrow.

I should just leave. I know it, but for some reason, I'm not getting back on my bike. I even light a cigarette, while I watch through the ER windows as she speaks to the nurse in the reception area. It's a short exchange after which Barbie goes to sit in the last row of the benches in there, right by the window I'm watching her through. Does she see me out here? Probably not. I'm in the dark where I belong, and I can only see her because of the bright lights in there and the fact that this is a small ass hospital that nothing much ever happens at.

Her and the nurse are the only ones in the waiting room, the parking lot is deserted, and the hospital above the ER area is dark. There's a bigger, more modern hospital near White Falls and that's the one everyone uses. This town is even smaller than my hometown, and even deader. I can't even hear any cars driving anywhere. I bet if I listened real hard, I'd hear people snoring in the houses nearby. I figured they'd take her right in. Why are they making her wait?

I should get on my bike and disappear into the night. I should do that before I start thinking about this situation too hard.

Because the image of her alone in the waiting room is already getting superimposed in my mind with what Roxie must've gone through when she was suddenly left all alone in this world. That's a new thing that I only started worrying about recently. The one I remember more vividly right now is how I raged when Lizard came to me with the lie that he found her, that she was his now.

I broke a couple of noses and smashed some heads in before they could overpower me. They fucking chained me up that night. Just like they would a dog. And once I stopped raging, I made the decision to survive every fight and wait for the opportunity to avenge Roxie and everyone else no matter how long it took. I held onto that hate and rage for years, but by the end I lost that connection too. I lost every connection to anyone I ever had, and none of them came back. Not even after I fucking disemboweled Lizard over what he'd done to my family. Not even after I sliced open most of the guys who helped him kill everyone I ever cared for.

But something like a connection is back now, as I watch Barbie sitting all alone in that waiting room. It came back before now, while I was still just checking her out at the bar, and certainly when I watched her get punched and couldn't stand for it.

If I leave now that boyfriend of hers will find her and give her a worse beating than the one she got tonight before he takes her back. The cops won't help her, hell, even this nurse won't help her. She's just letting her sit there, even though they clearly have nothing better to do tonight than take care of her wrist and her face. And Barbie's not the type of woman to beg for their help.

She's not even asking for *my* help. Not even after I added to the problems she was already facing.

And what, I'm just gonna leave now?

That cold well of regret and disconnection in the pit of my stomach is telling me to do exactly that. Leave, because she's not my problem. She's a club whore, I've known her type all my life, she just looks a lot better than any I've ever met did.

But I can't deny the connection. It's something I don't even get with Roxie anymore, even though she tries so hard. It's very lonely and dark in my head without something like it. And another voice is telling me that leaving her here will just be another thing I'll regret.

I don't know what that means, but I can call it what it is. And I do know I can't let her sit in there all beaten up and bruised, waiting until her boyfriend rolls by and takes her away for another beating. I probably can't keep her safe from him, but I can give it a shot. I can try to finish what I started.

BARBIE

FIGURES THE DREAM would be cut short before it got any better. That's what always happens with the good dreams. It's the nightmares that keep coming back.

This could well be an even worse situation than the one I woke up to today. I'm wearing a short, soaking wet red dress, no underwear, and a pair of pumps, and that's all I got to show for myself. Well, I also have forty dollars stashed in my bra, but that won't get me very far. In other words, I got nothing. And no one will help me get it either. Even this dumb bitch nurse thinks I'm trash. She keeps casting me glances that say that exact thing, while she doesn't let me in to see a doctor, even though I'm the only one in this waiting room. What does she think? That I deserve to be sitting here soaking wet with a swollen wrist and a face to match? She probably does.

I left her world—the world of normal people—behind to be wild and free and live out all my fantasies. But that sweet dream is awful hard to remember right now too.

The sliding door hisses open, but I don't even look up. Whoever came in will probably get treated first, and I don't need any more reminders of just how low I've fallen.

"What the fuck is taking so long?" Ice says harshly.

I look up automatically, ready to give him a piece of my mind about speaking to me that way, but at the same time my heart is fluttering in happy excitement, because he didn't just leave. I'm not completely alone after all.

He's not talking to me though, he asked the nurse that, and now the old bitch is just blinking at him, anger and fear both clearly visible on her face.

"The doctor's busy," the nurse finally chokes out.

"She's been sitting out here for half an hour with injuries you can probably treat without a doctor present," Ice says.

He's looking at me now, but despite the way he's standing up for me, I don't actually see any compassion or care in his face. But whatever, at least he's saying what he's saying, and that's more than any other guy's ever done for me. Especially the ones who made it necessary for me to come to the ER in the first place.

"Go wake the doctor and let's get this shit done," Ice adds.

"She...I...she'll just have to wait," the nurse says in a shaky voice.

"Go do it, or I will," Ice says.

The nurse gives him a very nasty look and mutters angry things under her breath as she leaves through a door behind her desk.

I walk up to him, and kinda just want to lean against him when I reach him, but I don't.

"She's bound to call the cops now that you yelled at her," I tell him. "We should probably just leave."

"But thank you," I add, as he gives me a once over. His eyes are strikingly blue and very, very cold. Like one of those winters that just won't end. Maybe his eyes are how he got his name.

He doesn't say anything, just squints at me and nods. It seems like he's struggling with something internally, like maybe the decision to come in here and help me, then take me somewhere where I'll have more of a chance to leave Brick behind. Because this ER waiting room ain't it.

"I'm happy you came back, that you didn't, you know, just leave me here," I say even though I don't actually know that's what he's doing. "Let's just get out of here. I don't need treatment, my arm'll heal. Look, I can move all my fingers just fine."

I show him and he looks down at my fingers. His face is still completely unreadable as he meets my eyes again, but the winter in his isn't as harsh, isn't as cold.

"You should get it checked out. You'll need your hand down the line," he says and I figure he's talking about sex now, because he's smirking, and because that's what most guys talk about when they're standing this close to me. But maybe I'm wrong. Maybe he genuinely just wants to see me get better.

"What's the problem here?" a bossy woman's voice sounds behind me.

I laugh out loud as I turn and realize it belongs to a tiny woman in a doctor's coat. She's more than a head shorter than me and half as skinny. I figured she'd be some large police woman or lady security guard judging by her loud and commanding voice. Laughing wasn't the best reaction though, because she's glaring at me even more angrily now.

Ice puts his arm around my shoulders and pushes me forward. "She needs to be seen."

The doctor's eyes narrow into slits as she glances at my injuries. She fixes her gaze on Ice right after. "And I suppose this was an accident. She fell down the stairs, right?"

"Yeah, why not?" he snaps back. "Now lets get this done."

The doctor keeps looking at him though, and she looks less and less confrontational and angry by the second. She's also not saying anything.

"Look, she got beat up earlier, I didn't do this to

her, but you do what you gotta do," Ice says. "Just treat her and make it fast."

"Let's just go, Ice," I put in since what he just said sounds too much like he still means to make me ask the cops for help, and not that he came back to take me along to wherever he's heading. "I'm fine."

"Ice?" the doctor asks quietly, blinking at him now. "Is that you, Brandon?"

That takes him by complete surprise, makes him look at the woman more closely and makes me jealous since a lot of that winter ice in his eyes disappeared. It makes no sense, and I blame the concussion, but I really want us to go now, so we can leave this woman in some distant past of his where she's obviously from and where she belongs.

"It's me, Mandy Ritter," the doctor says.

"Mandy Ritter, shit," he says, chuckling the way pleasantly surprised people do. "And you're a doctor now. Good going."

She still looks more shocked than anything else, and there's a fat gold wedding ring on her finger, so I doubt I have much to worry about, but I am.

"I thought you were dead," she says and the look on her face tells me she mourned him.

She said it with such a sad finality that it kinda shook me too, and the winter returns to his eyes like it never left. "Yeah, not actually. Look, can you see my friend now so we can get outta here? We're kinda in a hurry."

Doctor Mandy nods and asks the nurse to take me into the back, which the old bitch does right away. She's not muttering anymore though.

The doc doesn't come in to see me for a fat fifteen minutes though, and I wish I knew what her and Ice talked about during that time.

But what does it matter? He said we're leaving together after this, and that's all I really wanted to hear.

---

ICE

THAT WAS a stroke of luck running into Mandy here. Maybe things are finally starting to look up tonight. She was my closest neighbor growing up, and had the biggest crush on me from kindergarten through high school. It was kinda nice in a nerdy sorta way. She always let me copy all her homework and did most of my papers for me, so she's probably the only reason I finished at least part of high school. But she was always this skinny, tiny girl she still is and seriously not my type. She asked a bunch of questions about what happened to us that night and where I've been for all these years, but I kept it short and didn't tell her anything much. Except that Roxie survived, which she was real happy to hear like everyone is. I'm sure she'll keep quiet about seeing us here tonight.

But it still takes a long ass time before Barbie comes out of the ER with a shiny white bandage on her arm and a paper bag filled with pills by the sound of it.

"OK, that's finally done," she says as she reaches me. "Nothing's broken. Let's go now."

There's a bright shine in her face, like she's ready for an adventure. But that's probably just from the painkillers they must've given her.

I toss my cigarette into the bushes and shake my head. "Why you wanna come with me so bad? We've known each other for what, five hours? What if I'm some psycho?"

There's no *what if* about it, so I don't know why I even phrased it as a question.

Her face tightens for a second, because she's a shrewd woman who knows what's what, and knows I'm talking sense, but then she smiles very brightly, as brightly as she smiled at her old man earlier. Her eyes are glowing too, kinda like when the sun hits the ocean on summer mornings.

"You're not a psycho. You're a good guy, and I want to get to know you better," she says.

I laugh harshly at that, can't help it, since it's such a practiced line. She's a foxy patch whore, that's for sure. But she's also a very pretty one, and her smiles are warmer than sunshine.

"I'm not what you think I am," I say. "You're better off just walking away."

I don't know why I'm forcing this issue now. I stayed and waited for her because I want to take her with me. But there's a part of me that needs her to know that, because the rest of me knows it's the truth. I'm not someone anyone wants to get to know better. I'm not even a man anymore. I'm a ghost. A cold, revengeful, angry ghost. And she should be running away from me.

"Let me see," she says, biting on the fingernail of her index finger and looking up at the sky like she's thinking hard about it. "You took on five guys because one of them hurt me, brought me to a hospital, yelled at nurses and doctors because they didn't treat me fast enough, then waited for two hours while they mended me, so I'd have a ride from the hospital. If I sum all that up, you've already done more for me that any other man in my life ever has. Than all of them combined ever did, actually. And you did all that in the five hours that we've known each other. So yeah, I'm pretty sure I want to stay with you."

She gives me another bright smile once she finishes her little speech, and I don't know if it's her words, or her smile, but I kinda feel better and happier than I have in a good long while.

"Alright then, where do you wanna go?" I ask, since what else do you say to something like that? She's wrong, but she's hot and she's willing, and I'm no good at saying no to a good time.

"You're giving me a choice of anywhere at all?" she asks coyly.

I nod.

"Well, I've never seen the ocean," she says after thinking about it for a minute or so.

"A girl with ocean blue eyes and she's never seen the ocean?" I ask automatically, since that's the first thing that popped into my mind when she said it. "We gotta fix that. "

I point her in the direction of my bike.

"Good," she says and smiles over her shoulder as I walk a couple of steps behind her, enjoying the way her ass sways in that tight dress of hers. As long as I'm not looking at her bruised face, I still want to fuck her badly, even more than I did while she was sipping her wine at the bar.

It's a good plan all around. I'll take her to Cali,

show her the ocean and then take her to Sanctuary. The Devil's Nightmare guys will know what to do with her once we get there, she'll be safe from her old man with them, and I get to have her for the ride. It'll be a win-win outcome to what looked like a bad mistake just a couple of hours ago.

We might as well take the long way to Cali. I've been wanting to go cruising for a long time, and my ride out here wasn't as enjoyable as it could've been, since I knew what waited at the end. But the way back could be better.

6

---

Barbie

The last thing I remember is him helping me off the bike and leading me into a motel room. The sun was already up, and whatever they gave me at the hospital that made me feel real good right afterwards, yet knocked me out as soon as we rode away, still hadn't worn off completely. The afternoon sun is shining bright red through the flimsy curtains on the window and I'm alone in bed, still wearing my red dress, its strap pulling painfully against my bicep. The shower is running and his stuff is all over the room, so I know he didn't just leave me here again.

But knowing that did nothing to prepare me for seeing him walk out of the bathroom a few moments later, naked as the day his mother gave birth to him, only, well, a lot more grown up than that. If I had to point out a picture of exactly the kind of guy I want coming to me naked in bed, it'd be a picture of him right now.

He's muscled all over, like I already knew he would be from clinging to him on the back of his bike, only it's even better in the flesh. His sixpack has add-ons going off to the sides, his arms are all bulges and shapely lines, and his legs, well, they're strong and powerful enough to support any two people easily. I seriously dislike muscular guys with skinny legs and he's not presenting any such problem. But while all that is impressive, it's secondary, because, damn, his dick. I've seen my share of dicks, but this one—this one's the biggest I've ever seen. I wanna say it's beer can-sized, but that wouldn't quite do it justice. It's both fat and long, and I'm kinda afraid to even touch it, let alone allow it to get anywhere near my holes, but, damn, do I want it inside me.

My wrist's not throbbing anymore, and my head's not hurting either, both of which was a problem when I woke up a couple of minutes ago.

And I don't remember getting up from the bed to stand next to him by the bathroom either.

He snorts more than chuckles as I stop right next to him. "I see you're finally up."

"And I see you're not," I say with a smile and run my good hand down his chest and his stomach, but he grabs it before I can weigh that beast in my palm to see what I'm really dealing with.

"Take a punch to the face, run for your life all night, but after a good day's sleep you're ready for action," he says. "You're a good little slut, ain't you?"

The cold in his eyes washes over my chest, but he's not wrong. I want what I like and I think we both appreciate that fact.

"Don't pretend you don't like me." I extract my hand from his grip and keep going where I was going.

I gasp as my hand wraps around his dick, and so does he. And that coldness in his eyes isn't quite so freezing anymore, as I start to slide my palm up and down his shaft that's rapidly hardening under my touch.

He grabs me by the arms and twirls me around, pushes me against the wall, and the fast movement does make a sharp pain stab through my injured wrist, and a hammer blow go off in my head, but while he's rough, he's not too rough. His dick is still in my hand, and it's fully hard and pulsing now. I forget all the pain again as he yanks up my dress and spreads my legs open with his thigh. I'm not wearing panties because that's how Brick liked me, and he grins as he notices.

I can see he wants to kiss me as I look at him over my shoulder, and I can feel he wants to ram that huge, throbbing cock into me. It's all right there in his eyes, which are on fire right now, and in his coiled muscles as he holds me against the wall. Any second now I'm gonna feel that monster I fear inside me. And I can't wait. I even let go of it and arch my back out towards him, so he can do what he wants. My pussy is already wet and he hasn't even touched it. This will be one fun trip out to the ocean.

But instead of giving me his dick, he takes a step back and lets me go completely.

"Forget it, you're too banged up," he says and this rejection is colder and hurts worse than getting called a slut ten times over.

I turn around and glare at him.

"What? You're gonna act like that bothers you?" I can't exactly add, "or is it that you can't get it up," because it's clearly not true, but it's on the tip of my tongue.

"Stop being such a whore, and get cleaned up," he says. "I want some dinner."

"A whore?" I ask hiking my dress down as far as it goes. The pressure rising in my head is making it throb worse and worse. "You can call me a slut all you want. I am that, you knew it when you first saw me, and I own it. But I'm not a whore."

I can stand being called all sorts of things, but not that. That's where I draw the line. I've never taken money for sex and I never will.

"Calm the fuck down, Barbie, or you'll make your bruises worse," he says in an infuriatingly calm voice. It sounds like maybe he means he's gonna hit me if I don't, but that makes no sense, since he just refused to fuck me because I've got bruises on my face, and he beat up a stranger because he gave me those bruises. But what the fuck do I know about him anyway? I do know his type though, they like to give me bruises, so there's that.

"I'm not a whore," I repeat, since I don't know what else to say.

"Fine, I won't call you a whore, if it means that much to you," he says and walks over to the table opposite the bed where his clothes are. "But, I don't know, maybe you should stop acting like one, if that's your goal."

"What do you got against whores anyway?" I say, because I just can't let it go. He's really pissing me off with this holier than thou attitude. "I'm sure you've been with a couple before."

He's already got his boxers on and was about to pull on his jeans, but he freezes in the action and glares at me. "Yeah, too many."

It's not a joke or an offhand comment, he really means it, but I don't know how anyone can be with *too many* whores. I mean, it's a choice, isn't it? But he's completely serious, that much is plain in his face and in his dead, cold blue eyes right now. I have no idea how that can be, or how a guy like him can care so much about a small thing like fucking whores, since I've never met a guy with a big dick that didn't like to whip it out any chance he got just so he could brag about it later, if nothing else.

He didn't lie about having issues, because he's clearly got some of those. And the thing about guys with issues is that you never want to poke too hard at the walls they keep them behind. I learned that the hard way a couple of times over, and I stopped doing it long before today.

"Alright, Ice, I won't act like too much of a whore. I'll just toe the line between that and slut," I say and smile at him then slip into the bathroom before he can say anything.

Whore. Slut. What's the difference anyway? Yet I sure got worked up about it, and that's because I don't want this guy thinking of me as either of those things, for some reason. But he's gonna, how can he not? I shouldn't try to change that, because I also don't want this guy to turn into another Brick on me, or any other guy I was with before him. It's probably unavoidable in the long run, because they're all the same, but I want us to have some fun together first. I'm finally free again, and I mean to make the most of it.

ICE

"YOU ABOUT DONE WITH THAT?" I ask, even though I can clearly see she's still got more than half of her burger left. I ate mine fast, because the looks we're getting from the other patrons in this diner are pissing me off.

But who can blame them? Half her face is dark purple, her left eye is drooping shut and her arm is wrapped up in a bandage that's already not as clean as it was when they put it on at the ER about twelve hours ago. And she's wearing a tight and short red, evening dress while it's still light out. A dress, but no panties, and I've been thinking a lot about that.

That doesn't change the fact that she looks like a whore and I look like the guy who beat her up, and no one in here seems to like us being here very much. The waitress keeps giving me nasty looks, as does the middle aged lady at the next table, with her three kids that are making too much noise.

"Does it look like I'm done?" she asks with her mouth full, which is a totally gross sight, but kinda sexy at the same time.

I should've fucked her before when she wanted me to. Maybe I'd be in a better mood now. Because that hard-on she gave me isn't going away no matter what I think about, since anything I think comes right back to her not wearing any panties under that tight dress.

"Eat faster, I wanna get out of here," I tell her. "Then we can get you some new clothes and something to cover your face with."

She grins at me. "And then you'll fuck me? Once my face is covered, I mean?"

She hasn't stopped acting like a whore since I called her that, and it's seriously grating on my nerves. I should've fucked her. Don't know why I didn't. But the way she pounced on was a harsh reminder of those whores Lizard would bring to me in that cramped small room he kept me in. That made me feel even more like an animal than anything else. And I'm afraid they felt it. The memory she brought up was so vivid, I'm having trouble not seeing the twisted face of the last whore I fucked every time I look at Barbie. But thinking about her bare pussy under that short, red dress helps.

"Just hurry up, or else all the stores will be closed," I tell her.

"Man, you're bossy." She puts down her burger and wipes her lips. "I'm done. Do you want the rest?"

I take it and eat it in three bites, while she watches me with eyes wide in mock surprise. But I'm kinda done with her shit for today. I'm too used to being alone with just my own thoughts for company, and I like it fine that way. She just keeps talking and talking and doing weird things. Like right now, she's reaching down her dress into her bra.

"I mean to pay my own way to the ocean, just so you know," she says and tosses the money she fished from her bra onto the table.

I look at it and chuckle, which makes the food I'm not done chewing slam up into my nose.

"You're gonna pay your way to California with forty bucks, Barbie?" I say anyway, trying not to cough. "That won't even cover gas money to get us out of this state."

"Yeah, well, I'll pay you back for everything," she says. "Just don't take me for a whore."

There she goes again. It really bothered her getting called that, but I call it how I see it.

"Alright, Barbie, we'll figure it out," I say and wave to the waitress that I want to pay.

"Good, and, yeah, lets get out of here. I don't like the looks these people are giving us," she says as she watches the waitress approach. "What's this ass-backwards town called anyway?"

"Bixby, Missouri," I tell her as I pull my wallet out from my pocket. But she pays for the food with one of the twenties on the table, and tells the waitress to keep the change before I can do anything about it.

She gets up right after and heads for the door, while I'm still coming up with something clever to say.

It still doesn't come to me by the time we're standing on the sidewalk.

I hand her my wallet that I'm still clutching stupidly in my hand.

"Run along and get something to wear," I tell her and point at the strip mall across the street. "Better get a jacket too."

"And something to cover my face with, got it," she says, but doesn't take the wallet. "Aren't you gonna come with me to help me pick stuff out?"

I shake my head and force the wallet into her hand. "No, I'm gonna sit out here and enjoy the peace and quiet."

I'm also gonna enjoy her ass swaying as she heads across the street, which is what she's doing right now. I really should've fucked her before, because right now I seriously want to, and her not returning from this shopping trip is a very real possibility.

She's something else, this Barbie with the ocean blue eyes who's never seen the sea. Here she is all chipper and full of energy, cracking jokes left and right, with a banged up face and twenty dollars to her name. And she's stuck with me, the guy who hasn't felt joy since the last time I sliced a Spawn's neck open. She glows brighter than the sun, but I don't want to bask in her light, I want to put it out. And she doesn't know what she's up against here, she wouldn't be waving to me so happily from across the street if she did. She'd be running away. But I'm done warning her.

## 7

BARBIE

I GOT THE MAKEUP FIRST, since he's right, my face looks hideous. The old bruise Brick gave me is already turning green under the fresh one that's still mostly dark blue. I applied the foundation right there in the store, since I can do that in a matter of minutes after all these years of watching online tutorials about how to cover pretty much any kind of bruise or cut with makeup. But there's nothing I can do about my eye that's half shut. Though in my experience that'll be alright by tomorrow morning.

Ice gave me his whole wallet with over seven hundred dollars in it and just let me walk off. That made no sense to me when I first counted the money, but I figured it out while I was picking out clothes to buy. He probably did it so I'd have a chance to leave if that's what I wanna do. He's warned me I should often enough by now, and I'm starting to understand he's not the kinda guy who likes repeating himself more than once.

However, what he doesn't seem to understand is that I have nowhere to go, and he also doesn't know that I dreamed and daydreamed about leaving the place I was at for years. I didn't try to leave, because I figured wherever I ended up would probably be the same kinda shit in a different place, just like it's always been. But he's been successfully showing me there might be a better place out here for me, so I mean to stick around.

Right off the bat, he acted like a better man than any I've ever met before, and now he keeps doing it by giving me all this money, which is, more or less, enough to start a new life with. Especially for someone who's never had more than three-hundred dollars to her name at any one time.

That's how much I took from his wallet and stashed in the lining of my red dress after I changed out of it in the dressing room. I wanna stick around and find out if he actually is a better man than all the rest, or if what he's done for me was just a fluke, because he'd had too much to drink, and a play of circumstances afterwards. But I'm not completely dumb either, and I've been making my own way in this world for a long time. It's always good to have a Plan B.

But for now, Plan A is still looking pretty good. He's grinning at me as I walk up, and I'm glad I decided to wear the cut off jean hot pants I got instead of the normal jeans I also bought. I'm wearing just a tight tank top with them, even though the evening wind is damn cold and giving me goose bumps all over. It's gonna make me start shivering in a second, but for now that hot look of desire in his eyes is keeping the worst of its bite away.

"How's this for covering my face?" I ask once I reach him, turning my head to the side. I got the good makeup, which covered up my entire bruise. "Or where you thinking something more like a scarf?"

He shakes his head and grins even harder. I wish it did something for the winter in his eyes, but it doesn't. It's still colder than the ice age in there.

"I was thinking I'd give it another half an hour before deciding you'd split," he says. "And I was also thinking you'd get some warmer clothes. I thought you knew all about riding on the back of bikes. Winter is almost here."

*It's already here, as far as you're concerned.*

I don't say that. Instead I open the bag and show him the leather jacket I also got, along with some of the lacy kind of underwear I went a little wild on, since he gave me so much to spend. "I did get some warmer stuff, see. And I got boots."

I hike up my leg and place it on the back of his bike to give him a better look, though I'm sure he already noticed them. He likes seeing my legs spread open wide so close to him, I can see that despite that winter in his eyes. Or maybe I just feel it.

"I hope you kept the heels too," he says, which just makes me certain I was right. "Those were hot."

"And here's your wallet back," I say and hand it to him.

He pockets it without checking how much money is left inside. There could be nothing left and he doesn't even care. Just one more incredibly intriguing thing about this guy that I really want to figure out. I also really want him to be the one I've been looking for all these years. But that's a faded wish, because I wished it with every guy I liked, and I've given up on seeing it come true a long time ago. At this point, I'll just settle for someone who doesn't slap me around for every little thing I say or do wrong.

"Thank you," I add, belatedly remembering

what's left of my manners, but also because I really want him to know I appreciate all his help.

He grabs my ass and pulls me to him, so my pussy is pressed against his rock hard cock.

"How about you save the thank yous for when we get back to the room?" he says, and I don't like this roundabout way of him calling me a whore again. But I also really want to kiss him, because his lips are so close and he's still grinning at me, and I want to believe - no, I do believe - that there is more to our arrangement than that.

So that's what I do. Lean in and kiss him, moan as he grips my ass tighter and grinds his cock into me, sigh as he kisses me back. Because as he does that, our kiss starts to feel like I'm floating with the wispy summer clouds high in the sky, near the sun, lighter than air, and I don't feel the throbbing pain in my wrist anymore, or the dull pain in my face, or the headache I've had for the last two days. I just feel his hard cock throbbing against my stomach and his sweet soft lips against mine. I just feel good.

Then it's over, and he's telling me to get on his bike, and, yes, I do want to get back to our room. But I also want to stay right here and keep kissing him, because I don't remember the last time I enjoyed getting kissed more than I just did.

HE GRABS me by the hair and kisses me dirty and fast, as soon as the motel room door clicks shut behind us, pushing me back against it. But despite the wild roughness of it all, I'm as light as a cloud again, feeling things I've forgotten I could from just a kiss.

He's ripping off his clothes and mine, and I help as much as I can with my one good hand. It's all so dizzyingly fast, his desire for me like a freight train rushing through us both, and igniting mine. Just as I get a good grip on one sensation, another pops up, urgent and wild at first, lasting and fitting and simply perfect the next.

He's kissing me hard, causing my bruised up face to ache, but that's just one drop in everything else he's making me feel. Not even a big drop, just an inconvenience, because I'd rather be whole and complete and healthy for what we're about to share.

His hands are getting familiar with my breasts and my ass, my stomach and my neck, he's pushing me against the door, his tongue filling my mouth, tussling with mine as he gropes my soft parts. No part of him is soft. I know, because I'm touching most of them too. Sometimes our hands bump together as we're switching the parts we want to feel next.

Well, no part of him is soft, except his lips. Those are soft. His cock is rock hard, but the skin covering it is soft too, pure velvet against my palm. I'd love to taste him. He's breathing hard by the time his lips leave mine and travel down my neck, and so am I.

He yanks down my shorts without undoing the button or zipper first, the sharp tugging pain mixing well with the perfect bliss that's his lips on the soft spots of my neck, which is aching too, since Brick likes to choke me and that pain never goes away completely, but I'm used to it. And it's just a distant breeze on the wind tunnel caused by the freight train of our lust.

I yelp as he pushes at least two fingers into my pussy, but he silences me with another kiss. He hooks his fingers and starts pumping them in and out fast and wild, ravaging my pussy while his tongue assaults my mouth, and his other hand digs into the softness of my thigh as it keeps my legs spread. I'm so close to coming by the time his lips move down to my neck again, I'm only capable of making raspy, screechy sounds, even though the good way he's kissing my neck makes me wanna moan softly and sweetly.

Everything is just a burning mess of pleasure in

my mind and in my body, and I'm about to have the kind of orgasm I don't even remember ever having. It's almost here, I can almost already feel it, as clearly as I can feel the pulsing of his dick in my hand. I'm trying to stroke it, but can't because the mix of sensations in my body is already too wild, too unbearable, too much, and I don't have control over anything anymore.

Then they all vanish in a flash as he withdraws his fingers and stops kissing me.

But the next moment, I'm as light as a cloud again, ensconced in his arms as he carries me to the bed. All my aches and pains explode as he tosses me on the well-used, flimsy mattress, the musty, dusty smell of old linen rising around me.

That hardly registers in my mind though, because his body is covering me, its weight the perfect counter balance to my lightness, his smell the best I've noticed in a long time. It's leather and wind and clean like the clearest water, clear like ice.

"Slowly!" I scream out as he forces the head of his dick into my pussy.

With all the pleasure and bliss and fiery lust over-flowing in my brain, I'd forgotten how large he was, forgotten to fear it. But his massive dick is entering me like I've never been entered and he's not going slowly. All I can do is moan and gasp.

His cock is already so deep, but he keeps thrusting it even deeper into me, his face buried in my neck. The sweet, soft pleasure caused by his lips on my tender parts is less than a pop of sensation amid the ones his cock is causing in my pussy, my belly, all the way in my chest. That's pure fire. Welcome, all-consuming, but frightening at the same time.

"You're dick is so huge," I moan or shriek or yelp I don't even know.

He thrusts his dick even deeper as I say it, and looks at me as he does it, his clear, ice blue eyes the only thing I see as I come so hard, so viciously, so completely, I'm sure something inside me broke, shattered, but in a good way somehow. No part of my body is absent from feeling this orgasm, because it's impossible not to come on a dick this large, even when it's tearing you apart, even when you want it slow, even when you're a slut that's taken more dicks than I can count. It's impossible not to orgasm on a dick this huge, it's pure physics, but pure pleasure too.

My whole body is on fire, my blood carrying the heat and the sparks everywhere. He starts thrusting into me again, going deeper and deeper, and I'd moan and complain, but my voice has already been burned away by the fire. The only two things I know in this moment are that his dick is inside me and that I can't take it anymore. I can't come again, or I'll go mad, or I'll shatter too, just burn away into a pile of ash.

I'll pass out if he keeps this up. All the aches and pains in my body are amplified now too, and my pussy is screaming for a breather, for a rest, for all these sensations that the fire in me has raised beyond fever pitch to settle down again into something that won't kill me. I'm having trouble breathing already.

But he keeps his eyes fixed on me as he fucks me even harder, completely unfazed by the fact that my nails are digging into his flesh and drawing blood, as I try to make him slow down.

"Come, please come now," I whisper even as I do for the second time, my whole body just a massive, deep lake of smoking hot lava now. I'm gasping for air, which feels hot and sooty. The room is spinning before my eyes, but I see just enough to see him shake his head.

"I can't...no more...let me suck you off," I plead, my voice all broken and raspy.

And that finally stops his thrusts, where my shrieking, scratching and begging failed before. He removes his dick in one fast and jarring pull, then crashes down on his back next to me, sending the whole bed shaking. His cock is still rock hard, glistening from my juices, its pulsing visible to the naked eye.

The whole room tilts sideways as I lift up to do as I promised. Now that the fire in my blood is receding, and the burning is lessening in my brain, I'm just grateful for the orgasms he's given me, because they left behind a soft fuzzy cloud of pleasure in my belly, which is all my own. It's been awhile since anyone's fucked me this thoroughly and this well. I've been faking orgasms more often than not these last couple of years, and he's given me two mind-blowing ones in the space of...well, I don't know how much time has passed since we got back to the room, but I want to give him the same.

He groans as I wrap my lips around the head of his cock. My mouth is just barely wide enough to fit his girth, but he tastes fantastic, even despite my own juices all over him. I already knew he'd taste good, but being proven right stirs the embers, makes flames of desire rise high inside me again, so I get bolder, take more of him, take enough to gag.

"This ain't gonna work," he says and yanks his cock from my mouth, disappointed outrage now added to all the other things I'm feeling.

"I'll make you come real good, I promise," I say

and smile at him, which just makes him frown in an ugly way. Not the reaction I was expecting.

"No, you won't," he says and rolls onto his side, pulling the covers over himself. He's not even giving me a chance, and I'm an expert blowjob giver. I like giving head, it's my second favorite thing about sex.

I don't know what to say and I don't know what to do. I want to convince him some more, but I'm afraid to touch him now, because I'm pretty sure I'll get backhanded across the face on my first attempt at it. But I also want to finish what we started, and I don't want to just not speak and go to sleep now. I want his dick in me again. Just slower, less fierce, less wild, more perfect. And I want to taste him some more.

He's not moving though, and I don't feel him in the room as strongly as I did a couple of minutes ago, whatever that means. The runaway freight train of his passion has definitely left this station. That's what it means.

So I don't say anything and don't do anything. I just lay down and stay as still as he is, because I don't want to fuck this up, and because I have no idea how not to.

ISSUES. And, boy, does this man have some. I've been with guys who either couldn't get it up, or couldn't keep it up, and it's not a pretty thing to go through, but I've never been with a guy who could get it on this spectacularly, but then couldn't come. Or *wouldn't* come. I guess that's what happened. But either way, it's a first for me, a brand new thing to add to the long list of things I've already seen. Don't know why I'm even surprised, since pretty much everything about this guy is a first for me.

He's sleeping now, yet I can't. Every time I move I feel the devastation his dick left in my pussy, but that just reminds me of the pleasure he also gave me, and I want more of that, a whole lot more. After Brick started acting weird and kept demanding I fuck other men while he watched, it got to a point where I'd hardly feel them inside me anymore. I love sex, but that was demeaning and it made me forget just how passionate and wild and pure it could be. Ice reminded me very well tonight. And it could be so much better still, if not for his issues.

Here I am, back full circle to where this thinking that's keeping me up started. Back full circle to where every one of my relationships began and ended. They've all had issues. Every single guy I dated did. And I gave up on trying to fix any of their issues a long time ago, gave it up as a lost cause.

So why's this guy so different? Why do I go right back to thinking I should try to help him even as I decide—even as I know—that it's totally pointless?

It is pointless. He's fire hot one minute and ice cold the next. He's all nice one minute then rough and demanding the next. The winter in his eyes scares me, but I want to change it to spring. A pointless wish.

I could've left with his money earlier and been on my way to a new life now like I've been dreaming about doing for months. But I didn't. I came back here, all set on spending more time with him. All set on running away with him all the way to California. I'm no longer sure that's such a good idea.

All the running I've done in my life has been from the arms of one man into the arms of another. From my sleazy stepfather onwards. And it never turned out how I hoped and wished it would. Now I've just found a guy I thought could be better than the rest, but, as it's fast turning out, he's also got more issues than the rest.

That's my shit luck exactly. Should've seen it clearer from the start. Maybe I should just leave now.

I'm so sick of remembering all the ways my life is a complete and utter disaster, and I suspect I'll have plenty of time to do that if I'm on my own. It's easier to get lost in another adventure, with another man, one who at least has the power to surprise me, and who's nice to me more often than not. I also like how we just click most of the time. We clicked right from the very beginning back there in the bar. Maybe that means something.

But if he hits me, I'll split. This time, I'll draw the line at that and leave right after it happens the first time.

It's easier to doze off once I come to that decision. I want to get as far away from Brick and Razor as I can, and Ice is alright when he's not weird as hell. It could be worse, that could be Razor with his rotted teeth snoring beside me.

At least this guy's got a huge dick, and that goes a long way. He just needs to control it a little better. And I'm sure that's one issue I *can* help him with.

ICE

I SPENT six years fucking whores and wishing it was different, wishing I had the choice of finding and fucking a girl that wanted to fuck me, because she wanted to and not because she was paid to do it. And then I find one like that and I fuck her like I would one of those whores. Every which way I turn there's another reminder of how messed up in the head Lizard left me.

Instead of enjoying her like any sane man would, my mind shot me right back to that windowless, stuffy room where I fucked whore after whore until their faces blended together, and they all became just another outlet for the rage and the hate eating me from the inside out. She probably didn't lie about having no one else to turn to, but this set up we have going is too much like I'm paying for it. I'd blame her for coming on so strong, but my insanity is none of her fault and none of her doing. It's just all there is now.

The only difference last night was that I wouldn't stop for any of the whores like I did for her. Maybe that means something, but I doubt it. It just proves I'm a crazy bastard, because even after the crazy subsided, I still couldn't let her suck me off. I was too afraid it'd come back.

I woke up hating Lizard so bad I've been holding the knife I used to kill him, and wishing I could do it all over again, since well before dawn. It's light out now.

I'm not fit to be around other humans, he took that away from me and I let him take it. All I was still fit for after the Devils freed me was killing them all. And now that's done and there's nothing left. It's a bitter thing to swallow and just keeps getting worse. I should've left as soon as I woke up. Now it's too late again, because she's opening her eyes.

She blinks a few times, but her eyes widen real quick as she spots what I'm holding.

"What's with the knife, Ice?" she asks, her voice hoarse from sleep, but she sits up fast, as though she wasn't just dead to the world a second ago.

She's a beautiful woman, with perky breasts like two ripe apples and a taut hourglass shaped waistline. I'd enjoy her a lot if I wasn't this fucked up. I'd enjoy just watching her. However, I am this fucked up.

"Nothing to do with you," I say and toss the knife on the pile of my stuff by the door. "Get dressed. We're leaving."

She keeps watching me with narrowed eyes for a couple of seconds, then smiles brightly. Clearly, she decided I'm no threat to her. And that's her mistake.

"You don't want to come back to bed?" she asks and moves over to one side, making room for me. "The sun's not even up yet."

What the hell is she thinking? She wants me to fuck her again? Why? The scratches she gave me last night as she tried to get me off her are so deep they still sting.

"We better put as much distance between us and the two MCs I pissed off as possible. And as fast as possible," I tell her.

I can get her to Cali like I promised her. I can do that for her, but that's where it ends. Because having a good time ain't gonna happen for us.

"Pity," she says and smiles at me again, which I suppose is meant to make me reconsider, given how bright it is, but I'm not gonna.

"Get dressed."

"Alright, fine," she says and gets off the bed, showing me her perfectly round ass that's just as firm as those apple breasts of hers. I'd enjoy that ass too, once upon a time that I don't even remember very clearly anymore.

"But pity," she ads, glancing at me over her shoulder, which is damn inviting too. Back before, I wouldn't be able to resist her, and it's a bitter thing to know that I have no problem doing it now.

I'm done getting reminded of all the ways I'll never be who I was. Or wishing I could still have what I could've had if Lizard didn't come into my life.

Once we get to Cali, she'll make someone else happy with her smiles and her readiness to spread those fine legs of hers. And I'll just stay the fuck away from people—living or dead—after we get there. The ride'll take a couple of days, but we won't stop much.

"I'll wait outside," I say and grab my stuff, don't even put on my shirt before leaving the room.

I hope she doesn't take forever getting ready, because I want to get out on the road. That's the only reminder of my old life I can still stand.

# 8

BARBIE

WE'VE BEEN RIDING since we left the motel this morning, only stopping at a couple of gas stations in between. Now the sun is setting a dull orange in the distance, and I wouldn't mind stopping for the night, have a sit down dinner, maybe talk some more. He hasn't been very talkative all day, mostly just giving me yes or no answers to my many questions, and not saying anything at all when I was just talking and not asking him stuff.

That was kinda annoying, but I've also been holding onto him all day, and I'm more certain now than I was this morning that I want to talk to him some more, and have him talk back to me. And I want us to do other things together too. Maybe it's the steady rhythm of the bike lulling me into daydreaming about all this, or the fragrant, empty country roads we're travelling down, or the wind, which is warm, yet carries just enough of a cool edge to keep me awake and alert, so I won't miss even a second of seeing how beautiful the world actually is, how very big and vast it is, and how much of it is mine for the taking.

I love taking long rides, and I've been enjoying daydream after daydream, some of which even touched on the possibility that I finally found a guy I could share them with, despite last night, despite this morning, despite the fact that he hasn't uttered a full sentence on his own, since we left the motel. But all of that did happen, and it's much too early to be thinking anything of the kind. I do like this feeling that I *could* fall in love again though, I haven't felt that in years.

Seeing that knife in his hands when I woke up this morning scared me, but I believed him when he said it had nothing to do with me. His eyes were far away from the room we were in when he said that, so I think the knife has a lot to do with his issues. But I didn't dwell on that. I'll worry about it if he ever threatens me with it, and not before. I don't think he will. I hope he won't.

I always wanted to take a cross-country bike ride, but somehow I never managed to get very far out of Illinois. Maybe that's because I was always meant to take this ride with him, on the back of his bike, holding onto his waist, enjoying his smell and his presence, which begins to feel more and more like the one thing that's been missing from my life with each mile we cover, as the tires of his bike eat up the pavement and the clouds of evening gather.

Before settling with Brick, I've always been quick to fall in love. And out of it too. But this is ridiculously fast even for me, especially after thinking I'd never fall in love again for so long. Yet it's starting and I've never had any power to stop it. Nor ever wanted to. Love is the best feeling in the world. It's better than orgasms.

But my breath hitches as we turn a bend in the road and blue waters fill the horizon. We can't be there yet!

"Stop!" I tell him, then tap his side to get his attention when he doesn't answer.

"Let's stop!" I say louder as his eyes meet mine in the rearview mirror.

He pulls up onto the shoulder, because that's the

kind of guy he is. The kind that stops when I ask him to.

"What is it?" he asks as he turns to me. "You gotta piss?"

"Kinda, yes," I say and chuckle. "But I just wanted to ask...is that the ocean?"

I point at the water and he grins, smiling for the first time today, although it's more mocking than anything else.

"No, Barbie," he says slowly like he's explaining something to a child. "We still got more than two thousand miles to go before we get to the ocean. That's just a lake."

I laugh, mostly in relief that our adventure isn't over yet, but also because it's embarrassing he had to explain this to me. Now he'll be thinking I'm a dumb whore and I don't want him thinking either of those things about me.

"Well, I dropped out of high school and geography was never a good subject for me," I tell him.

"Yeah, I dropped out too, but I know where the ocean is," he counters and grins some more.

I shrug. "I'm a simple girl, a lake or the ocean, it's all good for me. Can we stop here and take a look?"

He smiled wider when I called myself a simple girl, but his face is tight again now. "I'd rather just keep going."

"What's the rush, Ice?" I ask. "I'm all shaken up from the ride, and my ass is about ready for a break. Come on, it'll be nice."

Guys like it when I talk about my ass, and I'm happy to see he's no exception.

"Alright, if that's what you want," he says and drives off again.

*If you want.* I haven't heard those three words in answer to my request in a very long time. And I like how they sound on his lips, very much so.

A few minutes later, he parks in a gravel parking lot that's almost empty. A simple wooden fence separates the lot from the lakeside, where a few people are walking, and an oldish lady is sitting cross-legged on a blanket, selling sweaters and scarves and such.

"Let's take a walk," I say and grab his hand the moment he's done stretching.

The world smells so clear and fresh right now, and that's probably just because I've been smelling exhaust and pavement dust all day, but it still brings to mind new possibilities, a different future, a fresh start like the kind I've made over and over in my life, but which lost all shine for me lately. It's shining bright this evening though. I didn't think I had another new start left in me, but right now, I think I do, and it's a very good feeling. It's glorious.

He lets me drag him through the opening in the fence, but then pulls his hand from mine. OK, so we're not ready to hold hands yet, that's fine, that will change. I'm smiling and he's not. That will change too.

"Would you like your palm read, young lady?" the woman on the blanket asks as we pass her, startling me, since I'm not sure I heard her right.

But when I look down, I see she does actually have a sign to that effect written in chalk on a small blackboard with the picture of a crystal ball drawn on it. It's sitting among a bunch of sweaters, cardigans and woolen scarves. From a distance, I thought she was Indian, but that's not actually the case.

"Sure, why not? That'll be fun," I exclaim, pulling on Ice's arm to stop him. "We can both get our palms read."

That kinda thing always scared me a little, since I'm just fine not knowing my future. My past is already quite enough to deal with. But today, getting the chance to find out what's in store for me feels like a sign, something I'm meant to do.

"I ain't getting my palm read," Ice says so derisively the lady gives him a very nasty look.

"Alright, just me then," I say and sit next to her on the blanket, offering her my hand.

"I need to see the left one," she says, then takes it in her warm dry hands when I offer it to her.

I glance back at Ice and grin, but he just rolls his eyes and turns to look out over the water.

"That's interesting," the gypsy mutters, trailing her finger along my palm.

"Oh-oh, should I be worried?" I say and laugh because she sounded very serious.

She fixes me with her gaze. Her eyes are so grey they're almost white.

"Your head line is strong and deep. You have no shortage of smarts or energy for living," she says and smiles at me, then looks back down at my palm.

"But your love line, I've never seen anything like it. It's very wavy and there's little tendrils breaking off it. " She traces the line she's talking about with her fingernail and looks into my eyes. "You've fallen in love many times but it never lasts, am I right?"

I nod and swallow the lump in my throat, which is preventing me from speaking right now. Can she really know this from just looking at these lines on my palm?

"And here..." She points at a spot on the line just under my ring finger. "Here it just disconnects and fades into nothingness."

I look at the spot she's pointing at, my heart racing. This is all bullshit superstition, but it makes so much sense right now. It explains exactly why love, the one thing I've been looking for has been so hard to find for me.

"But it starts up again here," I suggest, pointing where the love line on my palm starts up again after the gap. "It's not wavy anymore and there's no tendrils going off it."

It's also deeper than all the other lines on my palm, at least it seems so in this light, with the evening shadows falling on my skin.

"Hmmm," she says and falls silent as she peers at it, causing my heart to beat even faster in the silence.

"I'm not sure that's the love line continuing," she finally says and I don't know what to make of that.

"It has to be," I mutter, but she stays silent.

"You almost done here?" Ice asks sharply. "We should hit the road again soon."

The gypsy gives him another nasty look, but she's all smiles when she looks at me. "And your health line, that's nice and strong, young lady. You'll live to a ripe old age."

"Like my grandma," I mutter, and for once the memory doesn't bring just the bitterness of loss with it. "How much do I owe you?"

"Ten dollars," the gypsy says and Ice snorts behind me, but doesn't say anything.

I don't look at him this time, but she does, and I

don't much like the way her eyes turn even whiter while she glares at him.

I take my twenty from my pocket and offer it to her, forcing her attention away from Ice. She takes it and I pick up a thick, white, crocheted scarf that's as soft as cream despite its bulk.

"And how much for this?" I ask. It would be the perfect thing to wear on the back of the bike.

"You just take that," she says as she hands me a crumpled ten dollar bill in change. "You'll need it against the cold."

This time, her white eyes as they lock on Ice's, are so frosty they send a shiver down my spine. And I know she means him, that she thinks he's the cold I need to be guarded against. But she's wrong. He could be the one who's gonna guard me from everything else. I'm pretty sure of that already.

"Awesome, thanks! It's a beautiful scarf," I say and stand up.

My voice is all airy and light, and I'm smiling too, but she frightened me. As do his eyes once I take his hand to guide him along the lakeside for the rest of our walk.

He stops again when we're just a couple of yards away from the gypsy woman, who I'm now sure was just full of shit and wanted to get back at him for ridiculing her, with that talk of how I'm supposed to be wary of him. I mean, he deserved it, being so rude about her trade, but still, she was a bitch.

"Let's get back on the road," he says when I look at him questioningly.

"I thought we could stop for the night," I suggest. "I mean, we covered a lot of miles today. We don't even have to go to a motel, we could just stay right here. It's so beautiful."

And it truly is. The lake isn't blue anymore, it's awash in yellow and orange and all the other colors of the sunset sky. And the air is so clear and so crisp and so...

"We'll freeze," he says coldly, slicing right through the beginnings of another daydream come true in my mind.

"Come on, it's not that cold. You have that sleeping bag, I saw it, and we can build a fire," I say. "You must know how to do that, a far rider like you."

He frowns at me. "What the hell's a far rider?"

"I just made that up," I admit with a small little laugh. "I meant someone who likes to take long rides to faraway places."

He looks at me for awhile, his face calmer than the water behind him, and just as expressionless. He doesn't speak, looks out at the lake for a few moments, then at the road for a couple more, and then finally back at me.

"Alright, why not," he says.

I wish he sounded more excited about it, I wish his cold winter eyes would grow warmer in all this autumn beauty surrounding us, but I'm used to not getting what I wish for. And I'm good at making do with what I can get.

---

THE FIRE'S CRACKLING, the last of the day's light is just a narrow strip of yellow on the horizon, the breeze is making the black water of the lake ripple, and the air still feels like a new beginning is on the horizon. We could be kissing right now, I'd really like that. I still get lightheaded every time I remember that kiss we shared on the sidewalk. I get more than lightheaded when I remember the orgasms he gave me, but overall, the kisses didn't exactly lead to a very good conclusion to the night.

He's still checking me out like he wants me most of the time when he doesn't think I can see, but hasn't made any move to take me. I want him to, but I'm gonna let him make the first move this time around. The stars are starting to appear in the sky now, their reflections clear and bright in the water. The world is peaceful and calm and gorgeous. And it'd be very nice if he was at least holding me as we enjoy this gorgeous view together.

But he doesn't seem to be enjoying the view, and he's not talking again, and I'm starting to regret coming up with the idea to stop here. If we were riding, then at least I'd be holding on to him, getting lulled to sleep by the rumbling bike and the even, straight road. Instead, a foot of space separates us, and I'm not sure if I should try to get any closer than that, because I don't think he wants me to. It doesn't feel like he does, and I'm fearful of ruining anything happening between us before it even gets started.

Issues. Issues and baggage. I wish he could've just left all of that on the back of his bike with the rest of his stuff before we came out here. Because this could be so perfect without it. But he carries his problems with him at all times.

Maybe I should start talking about myself and then he'll open up too. Maybe that's the key here. I've been doing a lot of talking, and asking him questions he's not been answering, so I might as well give it a shot. I want to know more about him. I want to know everything and I want to know what I'm dealing with.

This is the night before a new beginning, the night when the old dies and the new begins. I'm pretty much certain of that. We're in the middle of nowhere, in the dark, lost to the world, no one knows where we are. We might as well not exist. Anything can happen on a night like this, and anything can be said.

"This is nice, don't you think?" I ask, chickening out again.

"Yeah," he says lazily. "You already said that a bunch of times though."

"Well, what do you want to talk about?" I ask. "You can tell me anything."

He fixes me with a long sideways glance. "Why do you keep asking all these questions? Don't you just wanna enjoy the silence?"

"I want us to get to know each other better," I counter. "It's a long way to California, like you told me before."

"Not if we ride hard," he says and chuckles coldly.

"I want to have fun while we do," I say, sounding too needy, but who the hell cares.

"You keep thinking you'll have fun getting to know me better," he snaps. "You won't. What else do I gotta do to prove that to you? Even that palm reader told you to stay away from me."

I gasp, can't help it, because that hard anger in his voice tells me he's gonna make me shut up, if I don't do it on my own, and I really don't want that. Not from this guy. He's done too many good things for me and I like being with him. He can't turn out to be bad like all the rest.

"Tell me something about yourself if you wanna talk so bad," he adds in a softer voice, echoing what I was thinking before I got cold feet, and once again proving just how well we click. "Or do I know everything already?"

He's talking about the whore argument we had yesterday, I'm sure he is, the way he's looking at me tells me that plainly, he doesn't even have to come out and say it. I don't like the implication at all.

"Yeah, fine, so I've been with a lot of guys, so what?" I snap.

"I figured you'd be sick of hearing their stories by now, that's all," he counters, grinning at me a little less mockingly.

"I never had a lot of choices," I say defensively. "I left home when I was seventeen, because my stepfather was getting too pushy. He started fucking me when I was thirteen, and he wanted to divorce my mom and marry me and all sorts of other bullshit. But he was too old and too nasty, and I was sure I could do better. My mother didn't care, the only one who cared was my grandma, but she got cancer and then she died. So I left, it was autumn then too, almost thirteen years ago. October 21st to be exact. It was a very cold autumn that year. It started snowing a week after I left. I remember that very clearly."

I have no idea why I told him all that. Maybe it's the dark, maybe it's so he'd stop thinking of me as just a whore and a slut who'll get with any guy. Or maybe it's because tonight's the night when the past dies.

"You remember that date very clearly. Sounds like you regret it," he says.

I roll up my sleeve and move my arm into the light, showing him the date tattooed there. October 18th. "This was the day my grandma died and I left right after her funeral. She was really afraid I'd turn out a junkie whore like my mom, right up until the night she died. But I promised her I wouldn't, and I kept my word."

He grabs my arm to get a better look at my tattoo, then glances at my face, his all tight and contorted.

"My mom was a junkie too," he says after awhile.

"It sucks, doesn't it?" I ask. He's still holding onto my arm, so I stay completely still because I like his touch.

He shrugs. "Don't remember much of her. She overdosed when I was six, and Pop never talked much about her after that. She wasn't a whore though, at least not while she was married to my dad."

"I stayed away from drugs all my life so I wouldn't turn out like my mom. I don't even drink much," I say. That was a very sad thing he told me, but at least he's talking. I guess.

"And what's that date below it?" he asks, running his thumb across it and causing sparkly shivers to run up my arm. Maybe this wasn't a bad idea at all. Maybe we're about to get closer.

"Is that the day you met the guy I took you from, the one who tried to sell you off to his buddy?" he adds, shattering my hopes of this night heading into a direction that'll make me scream in pleasure and not share sad stories.

I resent the mocking darkness in his tone, the way he's brushing past one of my saddest stories like I'm full of shit, like I'm just some whore whose stories don't mean shit, because she's worth shit. But tonight's the kinda night where anything goes. It's the kind of night when even the dead can be released. It actually feels exactly like the night I left my home to start a new life, and caught a ride with a guy that was the first in a long line of guys who were no better than my stepfather. Some of them were a lot worse.

"That's the day my baby died," I tell him and start

to pull down my sleeve again, but he's still holding onto my arm, almost gently.

"That's rough," he says and finally releases me. "How old was he?"

"My son was never born," I say, pulling my sleeve down all the way and crossing my arms over my chest. "Brick beat him out of me when I told him I was pregnant. But I wanted something to remember him by. I wanted to put butterflies and hearts around the date, but I could hardly stop crying for long enough to get the date on there. I'd also rather have the date of his birth on there, but I'll never know what that would've been, so I chose the date of his death. At least that I know. His birthday would've been sometime in the summer. Late June, early July. I really wanted to have my baby, because then I'd have someone I mattered to, you know?"

I never get choked up and I never cry anymore, but my throat is painfully tight by the time I finish speaking.

I didn't expect an answer from him, and I'm not getting it. He's looking at me from the side of his eyes, which aren't as cold as they usually are. I think. Because it's too dark, and I can't really know.

"In that case, I'm glad I gave him a good beating the other night," he says quietly. "I hit him hard, he's probably still recovering given his age, for what it's worth."

I nod because I can't speak. It's taking everything to stop myself from crying. I was wrong. Again. This is not the kinda night when you can let go of the past. A night like that doesn't exist. My past will always stay with me, and it will always hurt.

"I don't know how to comfort you," he says, and just the idea that he wants to eases the tightness in my throat.

"I lost everyone and everything seven years ago, and I lost my mind a couple of times over since then," he goes on in a cold and calm way, like he's just talking about the weather, and not sending shivers down my back. "I'm no good being around other people, Barbie. I shouldn't be, and I don't want to be. I can take you to California, but that's all I can do for you."

"I don't want much," I whisper, completely unsure of what else I could say to that. Though maybe I could tell him he's already given me more than I expected I'd ever get.

"I can't even give you a good time," he says and grins. "But I'll take you to see the ocean. Maybe you'll have better luck finding what you're looking for out West, near the ocean that matches your eyes, where the winters aren't so damn cold."

"Aegean blue," I interject stupidly, since the more he talks about not wanting anything to do with me, the more I want to change that.

He just frowns at me questioningly.

"Aegean blue, that's the color of my eyes," I elaborate. "I looked it up online once."

"Alright, Aegean blue, whatever the hell that is," he says.

"It's the color of a sea in Europe," I tell him, because I looked that up too.

"Yeah, we're not going all the way there. The sea in Cali is blue enough," he says and laughs warmly, which gives me hope.

"I'm sorry for what you went through," I say. "What happened?"

"It's a long, sad story and you got plenty of those already, no need to add mine to it," he says with finality.

"I got plenty of time," I say and smile at him. "And despite how much I talk, I'm also a good listener."

He looks at me, not saying anything, making me think he's gearing up to tell me his full story. Or kiss me. Either would be great. But he stands up and starts kicking dirt over the fire.

"Let's get back on the road," he says. "We got a long way to go."

He's almost put out the fire already, and I can't think of a damn thing to say to stop him.

I take his hand and try to make him sit back down anyway. "Come on, let's stay a little longer. There's no rush."

But he just shakes his head and puts out the last of the fire. It's cold now without its warmth and his iciness is making it worse.

He didn't get that name of his by chance. It's exactly who he is, and it describes him perfectly. And even though it's stupid and probably impossible, I wish I had enough fire in me to melt the ice around his heart, because I think that's a very good heart beating under all that frost, the kind I wish I could have, the kind I always longed to find. But I fear a fire that hot doesn't exist.

## 9

Barbie

"You know, I could go for sleeping in an actual bed tonight," I tell him as we pull up into a roadside restaurant, and I'm not just being cute saying it. After we left the lake, we rode for the whole night, then stopped for breakfast and rode some more. The sun is already setting. It was easier for me, I could sleep leaning against him, but I don't think he slept at all, not even during those few times we stopped and he found a bench or some such to rest on.

"Like at that place across the street," I say and point at the drab looking motel. "It looks comfy."

But then again, pretty much any place looks

comfy to me right about now, after spending more than twenty-four hours straight on the back of a bike. I have no idea how he does it.

He looks at the motel then frowns at me. "That place looks like a dump."

I can't really argue with that, so I just wrap my arm under his and lead him towards the restaurant. After a day and a night of holding onto him, it just feels natural to keep holding him, and he hardly even flinches as I do it. It must feel natural for him too.

We're in the middle of nowhere. The only signs of civilization for a bunch of miles it took us to get here, and for a bunch of miles onwards down this road, are this wood and metal sheathing burger joint, the shady looking motel across the street, and a gas station that looks like it was new around the time they invented the first car. I'm so tired and my whole body is vibrating with the rumblings of his bike even now that my feet are on solid ground.

"I want to lie down in a bed tonight," I say as he holds the door of the burger joint open for me.

I know what his first thought was when I said that, his desire shot through me like a bolt of lightning, but something much darker rode with it. But thankfully he stays silent as he follows me inside.

Somehow the interior is flooded with light. It's about half full of mostly guys, and they're all eating, so maybe this place isn't quite as far away from civilization as I thought it was.

"You're pretty used to taking long rides, aren't you?" I ask once we're sitting and he still hasn't said yes or no to my request. He must be tired too, but he doesn't really look it.

He shrugs, and picks up the menu, so I do the same. But all it says on mine is "burgers" and "beer". Seems like a waste of paper to print that shit out, but what do I know about running a restaurant?

I point that out to him and he chuckles, which is much better than the silence he's been meeting me with, but still not alright. Our conversations since we left the lake have been getting better and longer, but they're still pretty few and far between. I'm so tired and achy from the ride it's kinda pissing me off that he still won't talk to me much. This is gonna be one boring ride to the coast if we're neither talking, nor kissing, nor having sex.

"I guess I'll have a burger and a beer," I tell the waitress when she comes over. She looks half asleep and doesn't react to the mocking edge in my voice.

He gets the same—what else?—then rolls his shoulders once she leaves, wincing in the process.

"Yeah, I guess we might as well get some real rest," he finally says. "My shoulder is killing me.

Though I'm not a fan of these shitty roadside motels. I'm too old for it."

"And too rich," I add kinda too excitedly, but I'm so happy he's talking. And on his own too.

He just frowns at me questioningly. "Well, I counted the money in the wallet you gave me, didn't I? And that was already plenty. I figured there's gotta be more if you just handed it to me and let me walk off."

He grins, but it's not exactly a mirthful expression. It's too tight to be that.

"Yeah, I have more money than I know what to do with lately," he says and leaves it at that.

"I wish I had more money than I could spend," I say wistfully, although what I'm really curious about is where he got it. "I'd get myself a nice wardrobe and change my outfit every couple of hours. And my nails would always be done, and my hair would always be perfect…"

I keep rambling on, listing things I'd like to have, not even paying attention to what I'm saying. He seems to be listening, but when I get to the part where I ask how he got so lucky to get all that money, his previously slack expression grows hard like a brick wall in the second it takes me to say it.

He shrugs and points at my plate of food. "Eat, Barbie. Or your food's gonna get cold."

It's his way of telling me to shut up now, and I get that perfectly well. At least he's not mean about it like some of my exes would get when I talked too much. So there's still that.

I don't feel like talking anymore anyway. I'm sick of just listening to the sound of my own voice, which is pretty shrill by this point anyway, since, damn it, how do I get this guy to say more than two sentences at a time to me? How do I get him to kiss me again? He watches me like he wants to when he doesn't think I notice, but otherwise, he's been as cold as, well, ice, towards me since we left that first motel we stayed at.

Maybe we can change all that at this new one we're staying in tonight.

---

"I NEED A SHOWER," I say as soon as we're inside the motel room, which looks a lot cleaner than I imagined it would be. It kinda smells clean too. Like bleach, but clean.

"Yeah, me too," he says dumping the saddle bags he took off his bike on the floor next to the door.

"You're welcome to join me," I say and smile at him invitingly over my shoulder as I head for the bathroom.

But he shakes his head and turns away, which is disappointing to say the least. And frustrating as hell.

I don't get a much warmer reaction when I come out after my shower, wrapped in the smallest towel I could find that still covered most of me, and with my hair dripping wet.

He brushes past me as he enters the bathroom and he didn't have to get so close, there was plenty of room. That gives me hope. But he did pass me, so it could just be a false hope.

"Try not to jump on me when I come out, OK?" he says grinning at me through the almost closed bathroom door, raising my hope sky high again.

"Don't walk around naked, if you don't want me to want it," I counter, which makes him grin wider.

"That's something guys say to women, Barbie, not the other way around," he says to which I just shrug, since he's perfectly right. But I smile too, because I meant it.

He closes the door, before I come up with any more clever lines. But I guess it's a start, and we always gotta start somewhere. I should know. I've been through plenty of starts. False ones, sure, and that's what this one very well might be. But a start is always better than an ending.

I removed the bandage from my wrist before I

took my shower, since it was almost black from the road dust and because I need both hands to carry out my plan for tonight. The swelling's gone down, and it's loosening up nicely, there's almost no pain left when I move it around.

He comes out wearing just a towel around his waist, before I even decide what to wear to bed. I didn't get anything to sleep in when I went shopping, figuring I'd be doing all the sleeping naked anyway. Not how it turned out, but maybe I can still turn it around.

He's squinting at me like he'd like my towel to fall just as much as I'd like his to do the same. He's a fine looking man, head to toe, and I'd love to have those bulky, strong arms of his wrapped around me. I've done a lot of daydreaming about it, while I kept mine wrapped around him on the way here.

"If you're shoulder's still bothering you, I can massage it out for you," I offer. "I'm pretty good at that kinda thing."

He could say something mean to that, could mention that I must've had a lot of practice at that for sure, but he's still just grinning and squinting at me like he's waiting for my towel to fall.

"Yeah, sure, why the hell not?" he finally says. "It's the right one, and it's fucking burning."

"Lie down then," I say and smile at him while I fish the lotion from my plastic bag of stuff.

He eyes the bottle and then me, a touch of that meanness I expected long before now coloring his eyes. "You're prepared."

He leaves it at that, and I sigh in relief before telling him again to lie down. This time he does, on his stomach on top of the covers, only pulling out one of the pillows to get comfortable.

A massage isn't all I have in mind, but I figure his hard-on, which was already tenting up that towel before he laid down, will get painful soon enough, and then he'll turn around on his own.

I drop my towel, since it keeps slipping off anyway and there's no need for me to go through the bother of adjusting it every two seconds, given that he's got his head buried in the pillow. I better make this fast, or he'll go to sleep on me.

I straddle his hips, and he groans a complaint quite unnecessarily, since I'm sure I weigh nothing to him and besides, I'm not putting my full weight on his back. Maybe he's just groaning because my clit is touching his skin. Hell, I even moaned a little. For such a cold guy, his skin is nice and warm, and I like that in a man.

His back is just one muscle atop another, all braided together in an intricate pattern I can't wait to unravel. He doesn't have a lot of tattoos, I expected his back to be covered with some, but there's not a single one here, and the ones on his chest and arms are few and far between too. I wonder why that is. He's gotta be in his thirties. I'd expect a guy like him to be covered in tattoos by this ripe age. Maybe he doesn't like needles. But he doesn't exactly strike me as the type of guy who's afraid of anything. Except himself. He seems to be afraid of himself.

"I'm waiting," he mutters, snapping me out of my mesmiration with his back.

"Yes, yes," I say and dump a good heap of the lotion onto my palm.

He inhales sharply when the cool liquid comes into contact with his burning skin, but it soon turns to groans of pleasure as I get to work.

I have long, deft fingers that are pretty strong too. Soon enough I get lost in finding the knots in his muscles, coaxing them out, and unraveling them slowly. I wish all the knots keeping us apart would be this easy to unravel. But I lose that train of thought too, as only the feel of his tight muscles fills my mind. They're hard yet pliant under my fingers. I've been daydreaming about touching him for two days and now I finally get to, and that's all that matters.

There's a large scar running from the top of his right shoulder down past his shoulder blade. It looks surgical and it looks old, but I assume the injury that made the cut necessary is the cause of his pain. He's got other scars too, along his ribs and near his spine, but they're smaller.

I left his shoulders and neck for last. His groans of satisfaction get louder once I finally settle on his shoulder. It's full of knots, harder than the rest of his muscles were.

"You had surgery here, didn't you?"

He just groans a yes, and doesn't take the bait to start talking. That's perfectly fine though. My burning need for him to talk to me is not as hot now that I'm touching him. Which is something I could do for hours and not get tired of it at all. My wrist isn't aching at all despite how hard I'm pressing down on his back.

"You're really good at this," he says, after I was pretty sure he'd already fallen asleep.

"Yeah, I know," I say. "And I know what you're thinking too. You're thinking I'm so good at it because I've done it many times before, to many different guys. But I'll have you know, I never liked touching a guy as much as I like touching you."

"And I bet you said that to every single one of

them," he says and laughs, but not meanly and that's a start.

"If I did say it to anyone else, and I don't remember doing it, then I was lying," I say and that's God's truth.

He doesn't say anything to do that and I guess that's better than some mean comeback. But I've also touched every inch of his back several times over, and I want to explore other parts of him now.

"I can see why this shoulder is killing you," I say, finding yet another knotted part in it. "That must've been quite a fall."

I figure he got it in a bike accident.

"It was a kick and a fall, actually," he says after I already didn't expect him to speak. "But I still won that fight even with my right arm useless for the last round of it."

"You've been in a lot of fights, haven't you?" I ask. I pretty much figured that out on my own by now. His nose has been broken a few times, and he's got scars on his face, which could only be there from fists.

"Yeah, a lot of fights and then some," he mutters. "But I won every last one of them in the end."

The way he says it sounds like he's talking to himself not me, and it's eerie, it's surreal and gives me the shivers. And that's not how I want this evening to play out.

I give his shoulder another good squeeze and then let go, sliding off him. "Turn around now, let me give some attention to the front of you too."

He chuckles, and I'm sure he's gonna say something else clever then go to sleep, but he surprises me by flipping around, the towel around his waist falling open on it's own. He must've heard my actual suggestion between the lines, since it's been my experience that guys hear "blow job" even when it wasn't actually hinted at.

I grin at him, struggling to keep my eyes locked on his, and away from his raging boner. He grins back, so I lean down and kiss him, but that electric connection of ours I've been longing to feel again for two days only lasts a split second. He pulls away and stops me from going for a second try with his hands firm on my shoulders.

"I don't wanna start anything I can't finish," he says, and I know he's not just talking about my failure to make him come the other night. But tonight, I'd like to keep it real simple between us.

"How about we not worry about finishing before we even start?" I say and grin at him.

He narrows his eyes, but he understood me

perfectly well. And I think that gleam in his eyes means I've finally managed to drag him onto my page of how this adventure of ours should be unfolding.

"Alright, Barbie, let's do it your way," he says, and this time he doesn't stop me from kissing him.

He kisses me back, his fingers getting tangled in my wet hair as he strokes my head, his tongue and his lips making sparks of pleasure radiate all through me like waterfalls of electric starlight, filling me with joy and hope and desire. I'm a simple girl and I don't know much, but I know he and I were meant to kiss each other. Because I've never been kissed this good before.

And tonight, I will make him come.

So despite wishing this kiss would go on forever, I pull away from his lips and trail a string of soft licks and kisses across his chest and the hard bumps and valleys of his stomach, and even across the scratches my nails left when he gave me more than I could take. I ignore those as I kiss my way down to his dick, the taste of which I kinda missed. Actually, really missed.

He's all tense now, his muscles coiled and taut, and I can feel that more than see it. He radiates power and strength, and I can understand how it could be that he won every fight. But he doesn't have to fight now. I'm about to make him feel amazingly good.

He sighs hoarsely as my lips envelop the head of his cock, and I moan too, because I've hungered for this for a very long time. I'm not even sure what it is, but, somehow, he fills something inside me that's longed to be filled for so long I didn't even know it was missing, until I got my first taste of it. That's how everything between us has been—just exactly right from the get go. Everything he did for me and to me, showed me what I've been missing, what I've forgotten I missed.

I always liked giving head, but this goes beyond mere liking. I take more and more of him, let him glide down my throat, moan as the tender skin of his dick slides back out, my tongue rough compared to his softness, but perfect too, just right. He bucks into my mouth a few times, his hand a fist in my hair, but then he relaxes, as I ignore all that and continue at my own pace, in my own well practiced way. Soon, the fight leaves his body, making it soft and malleable, mine to control and please.

He's close, I can feel it as his balls tighten and his cock grows even larger in my mouth. I want this to last a little longer though. I'll never get enough of the taste of him, and I certainly haven't had enough yet tonight.

So I slow it down like I know how to do very well, suck on his balls for awhile, then just on his soft head, lock eyes with him as I lick the pulsing vein that sends a volley of tickles from my lips to my chest. His eyes aren't cold and hard anymore, and I see deep into them, see the guy I know he is, and not the guy who's trying so hard to keep me at a distance.

Finally I take mercy on him, because I know he wants to come, I know he needs to, and I know he's about to have the orgasm of his life. I am that good at giving head.

I speed up my licks and my bobs, play with his balls the way I played with his back before, only gentler. Before long his whole body grows incredibly tight and extremely taut again. I just keep going, moaning as I do, enjoying this as much as he is. He comes with a long hoarse groan that sounds like fabric tearing, and fills my mouth with his semen, with so much of it, I have no hope of swallowing all of it, but I do my best. Because he tastes fantastic, right to the end, through and through. I don't even have to breathe, just this is enough.

"You're so fucking good at that," he says as I look up at him.

His eyes are two very narrow slits and there's no

meanness behind his words that I can see. It's just a simple thank you.

"Come here," he adds, and makes room for me beside him on the bed.

But then he falls asleep before he's even done wrapping his arm around me.

That's OK though, that's just fine. So I just pull the covers over us both and turn off the light before getting real close to him and resting my head on his chest. Now this is what I call a start.

ICE

I DIDN'T MEAN to just fall asleep, and that's my first thought when I wake up in the dead of night with Barbie sleeping soundly in my arms. But it was beyond my control, because that was one hell of a blow job she gave me, I've never had better. I should let her sleep, but I don't remember the last time I was as horny for a woman as I am right now. And the source of it, the cause of it, is lying naked in my arms, and she's more willing than any other woman I've ever been with.

I've been riding fast, refusing to stop for more than an hour at a time, to get away from that too.

Because I'm not right in the head and she deserves better. Her telling me the sad fucking story about her dead baby just solidified that knowing in my brain.

Yet, she's gorgeous and willing and I want her. It's been a long time since I wanted anything other than death. My own and that of the men who made my life the hell it was and still is. But now I also want Barbie a lot.

I wanted her from the moment I noticed her, but that got real complicated real fast. Despite my silent gruffness these last couple of days, which didn't work to keep her quiet like I figured it would, I enjoyed listening to the sound of her voice. I also enjoyed her hanging onto me on the back of my bike like that's the only thing she wanted to be doing. And that's all that really should matter.

I want to make her feel good, the way she makes me feel good. That idea is foreign to me, it's like an echo from another life, from somewhere far and deep in my past, from the life I'll never get back. But it's a very loud echo right now.

BARBIE

A SHARP BITE and tug on my nipple wakes me, but it's followed by the best neck kiss I've gotten in a long time, landing right where it feels the best and sending a rush of pleasure running like an electric river straight down to my clit.

I open my eyes to see Ice grinning at me, his lips inches from mine. "I didn't mean to just fall asleep before."

I grab the back of his head with both my hands, his prickly shaved scalp rough against my palms as I pull his lips that last inch to me, and kiss him, because the river of pleasure is already waning and I need more. I'm so thirsty for the electric torrents of pleasure only he can give me.

But he's not satisfied just kissing the way I would be, even though that's not usually the norm for me. Then again, no one kisses this good, at least no one that I've ever met.

The room's bathed in a similar yellowish light that covered the lake we stopped at the other night, but this one is coming from the street lamp outside our window, because the room is dark otherwise. I'm writhing and moaning on the bed as his lips travel first down to my neck, spending some time there and making the sparkling rush of the waters of pleasure overflow inside me. Then his lips and teeth find my nipples again. He takes one between his lips, sucks hard and pulls, makes me yelp and whimper, which turns into a long moan as he kisses it softly. He does it again and again, and I'm coming off the bed in my combined need to get away from the intensity of the sensation and my need for more. His kisses leave none of me untasted.

He knows how to make a woman feel good, I'll give him that, and I knew it the first time we were together, but this is so different than that first night. It's just as intense yet less urgent, the freight train of desire that ran us over the last time just a hint on the horizon. It's been awhile since my body was worshiped this good, and it's been longer since I could give myself this completely to a man's touch, this seamlessly. I'm not just floating on clouds this time, my brain is all clouded over with the pleasure he's giving me. Brick never had much time for making me feel good, or much inclination to do it. I had to take what I could get from him myself. This is nothing like that, I can trust Ice to do what needs doing and I can just let go and enjoy. My pussy is good and wet by the time his kisses reach it.

He knows how to use his tongue down there too, which isn't the case with most guys. But he finds my bud with the skill few possess and by the time he adds two fingers to the mix, opening me up and hitting the exact right spot inside me and out, I can't even fully remember any other time another guy went down on me. Those times are just faded, fuzzy memories right now.

A couple more jabs, a couple more licks and kisses, and then all I'm aware of is this rush of the electric rivers of pleasure about to consume me. A few more jabs, a few more licks and kisses and I'll be done. The end comes quicker than I expected. The roiling river of pleasure breaks its bank, rushes every last nook in my body and soul, fills it with sparkling electric sparks exploding inside me like fireworks made of pure gold and light and fire no water can ever douse. I come so hard I'm seeing two of him, two of us, and he's just as gloriously yellow as that sunset by the lake. Only more beautiful, because he's real and he's here giving me this bliss, while that sunset was just a passing thing. I see him clearly even after I close my eyes.

"Hey, don't go to sleep just yet," he says, but I can hear the smile in his voice.

And when I open my eyes I see it too. "I wasn't gonna."

He's leaning over me, his rock hard and huge erection pulsing against my clit, which is still throbbing from the orgasm he just gave me.

And I can feel that freight train of lust that ran me over last time getting dangerously close again.

"Let me get on top, big boy," I say, gliding my hands down his sides, my fingers bumping against the scratches I left there the last time he lay over me like this.

He groans as he rubs his cock over my clit, making me moan and think he's gonna say no. But then he grins at me and gets off, crashing down on his back beside me, making the bed bounce and creak.

"Alright, get your fine ass over here," he says.

He likes looking at my ass, I've noticed that during the last couple of days. So I'm gonna give him a good view of it as I ride his cock to my next orgasm. And his too, because I won't be satisfied with any other outcome tonight.

I nearly get mine the moment I sit down on his cock the reverse cowgirl way, and that's just from the first couple of inches entering me. But I bite down hard on my lip and stop for a second until the wave passes, because as much as I like sex and coming, I won't be able to stay awake after another hard orgasm like the one he just gave me.

Once it passes and I start sliding up and down his shaft slowly, rhythmically, rolling my hips and stroking his powerful thighs, letting the waves of pleasure roll over my body and soul softly and lastingly. Their ends are already igniting with sparks of electric pleasure, which will soon consume the soft rolling waves, and me. But I mean to make this last first.

He's big, but not too big if I take him like this, at my own pace, letting in just a little more each time I come down. And each time I do that, his cock hits yet another pleasure button inside me, a place I didn't know was sensitive until he showed me.

His hands are on my hips, but he's not guiding my movements, just following along as I ride the waves of pleasure, explore all the layers and depths of this wavy sea of bliss that goes deep, that coils and roils, rises and falls and takes me on its current, lets me float, doesn't drag me anywhere.

"That's a real nice butterfly you got there," he says hoarsely, referring to the tattoo on my lower back.

I look at him over my shoulder and smile, gyrating my hips up and down just so, moaning as I do because I can't help it.

"Doesn't it look like it's flying when I do this?" I ask, even though it's hard to string words together into a sentence. His cock feels too good inside me.

"Yeah, it sure does." He grins mischievously, but not meanly. "Why don't you turn around now, I wanna watch you come."

I smile wider and spin around on his dick, which wipes it right off as a I very nearly give him what he asked for just by doing that alone. I'm sure it's not the prettiest expression I could be wearing, and it takes me a few deep breaths and a hard bite on my bottom lip to settle down again.

He laughs as he brings his hands up my stomach and cups my breasts. The sharp pain as he twists both my nipples at the same time clears the rest of the fog my almost orgasm brought.

"Is that better?" he asks. I nod, since I can't speak just yet.

"Alright, now show me what you like," he demands.

He's a completely different person than he was that first night he fucked me. Tonight he's the man I wanted to feel inside me, over me and under me from pretty much the moment my eyes met his in that bar where he prevented my worst nightmare from coming true, and every day since.

I smile at him as I start sliding up and down on his cock again. I'm going slow, twisting my nipple and sucking on my thumb while moaning sweetly, giving him a show, but taking him the way I want him.

I'm lost in his eyes, where the sun is finally rising above all that wintery ice, and I can see very, very far, all the way to the end, in them. But that's not true either, there's no end in his eyes, just a slow road to forever, and I want the ice to melt, turn into rivers like those his kisses and his dick and his kindness let loose inside me.

I don't know what he sees in my eyes, but I hope it's what he wanted to see too, because I can't hold out any longer, I need to let this wavy sea of pleasure wash over me now and take me under, drown me in its blissful, electric, everlasting depths. I can hardly breathe anymore as it is, and I need this release.

The ice in his eyes sparkles as I come, everything sparkles as though the sun is high in the sky, shining down on us, illuminating, warming, revealing and healing every inch of my body and soul, and every last piece of my heart, which I haven't seen or felt this clearly in a very long time.

He comes too, seconds after me, completing the circle of light and bliss, of sparkling pleasure that takes my breath and my sight. But I don't need to see and I don't need to breathe, I just need this electric connection of ours that we've finally forged completely.

## 11

ICE

SHE'S LYING in my arms, her head resting against my shoulder, her fingers twirling the hair on my chest and her naked body soft and warm and kinda sticky where it's pressed against me. I always liked this part of sex, just lying with the woman afterwards, spent and satisfied, and I always got a lot of shit for it from the guys I rode with if I talked about it, but that didn't bother me and it didn't change it. Women feel good to have around any which way.

That said, there was never just one for me, it was a series of club whores and random chicks I met on the road, but they all felt good. All of them, until the whores Lizard brought to me. One by one, those made me forget how good women felt in my arms and on my dick and on my bike. But Barbie, she makes me remember, and those memories are more than just echoes right now.

"You have so few tattoos," she murmurs. "How come?"

She's tracing the one I have over my heart with her fingers, the one of my father's club colors — of my club's colors, the Wolves of Hell MC. It's faded, because I got it a long time ago, long before it all fell apart. And I don't much like the echoes her question brought up now.

At first, I figured she already knew who I was, being such a club hanger-on, and that she was just tactful by not asking direct questions about it. But she just kept asking, which led me to believe she didn't know. It was refreshing not having all that shit from my past hanging between us the way it always hangs in the air wherever I am and who ever I'm with. Her not knowing also kinda let me not think of it so much.

But what does it matter if she knows my whole story? I'll never forget it anyway.

"For a long time, I wasn't free to just go out and get a tattoo whenever I felt like it," I tell her. "And that was the case until very recently. Nowadays, I don't much care about shit like that."

"Then what do you care about?" she says and lifts her head to grin at me.

"Nothing," I tell her truthfully, and she doesn't like that answer, I can see that plain in the frown on her face. She believes me though, I can see that plain in her *Aegean* blue eyes too.

"What the hell happened to you, man?" she asks and lies back down on my chest like she's not expecting me to answer.

What the hell difference does it make if I tell her? At least she'll stop bugging me with questions if I do. Hopefully.

"Seven years ago, my entire MC was destroyed by a rival club—Satan's Spawn MC — you probably heard of them, they ran that whole area you played around in for a long time. Over two hundred people dead in one night, all the members, all the club whores, the old ladies and their children too. It was brutal and unnecessary."

She flew up the second she started comprehending what I was telling her. Now she's staring down at the tattoo on my chest with her palm across her mouth and her eyes very wide. And sparkly. I like how her eyes sparkle.

"Wolves of Hell MC, that was your club, right? I

remember now," she mutters, still holding the palm over her mouth. "It happened before I came to town, but I heard stories."

I shrug, since what the hell more is there to say? I'd prefer to be kissing her right now, but all these memories telling her brought up and the hate they carry are fast making an echo of that wish.

Her eyes get even wider like she just remembered something else. "Brick called you Iceman at the bar."

I nod. "Yeah, so I thought you knew all about me."

"I didn't really follow that conversation all that well at the beginning. I was struggling to stay conscious," she says, finally taking her hand away from her mouth and laying it over my heart.

The bruises on her face are almost gone and she keeps them covered with makeup pretty good, but they're enough of a reminder of why I saved her that night to make even the hate recede a little, and keep me in the present, not in the rain on my knees on that dark night when my life ended.

"And even after I started remembering all the pieces of it, I still didn't put two and two together," she goes on, I guess heading towards the part where she tells me she does in fact know all about me. "You're *the* Iceman, the Death Match Champion, right?"

I nod and I kinda like the awe in her voice, and the fact that I like it.

"Seven, a guy I dated told me all about you," she continues, and the hate hearing that brings, nukes every good thing I was feeling a split second ago. "I even watched you fight a couple of times."

She pauses to take a ragged breath, since all that talking seems to have knocked the wind out of her. Kinda like her telling me that Seven fucked her did for me.

"Seven said you betrayed your own MC and helped the Spawns kill them all, so that you could fight for them in the tournaments," she says. "Something about your father not letting you compete, and that's why you got rid of him."

I chuckle which makes her gasp like I frightened her.

"Yeah, they liked spreading that lie around. It's true that my father didn't want me to fight, but also that I did fight for years despite it. Lizard knew that and he wanted me to fight for him. It's why he didn't kill me that night along with everyone else. And I'd never harm my father, I loved and respected him," I tell her, and it feels good hearing it. "What really happened was that the Spawns took me prisoner and then kept me locked up, only letting me out when it was time for another fight."

I'm seeing the moment I killed Seven very clearly before my eyes. So clearly, Barbie fades into the background. I hate knowing she fucked a Spawn, but Seven probably wasn't even the only one. She gets around. I'm trying to hold onto the knowledge that she's just a girl, alone in the world and with nothing, just trying to make it through this life in any way she can, but it's not helping. The fact that she's not saying anything, where she won't shut up usually, isn't helping either. But what's there to say to something like what I just told her?

"I never liked Seven very much, or any of the other Spawns I met," she says. "There was what they did to your club, but they were also just a nasty bunch of guys all around."

"Well, they got theirs now," I tell her. And I gotta admit that what she just said was probably the perfect thing anyone could've said. But that's just Barbie. She talks a lot and she knows what to say.

"And you'll never have to keep their company again," I add.

She's still very wide-eyed, but she nods when I say that. "I heard that they were all killed. Did you do it?"

There's fear in her voice, but not nearly as much as I expected. And not nearly as much as there should be. I didn't just kill off the Spawns, I enjoyed doing it, and I'd enjoy doing it all over again.

"I had help, but yeah, I got most of them," I tell her. "Seven was one of the last to go. He was a spiteful, arrogant bastard right to the end."

His old lady got killed because he wouldn't back down, not even at the very end, but I can't say I felt particularly sorry about that turn of events. And I still don't.

"Yeah, that's the guy I knew too," she says. "They got what was coming to them, I guess."

And there she goes, saying the most fitting thing again.

She lays back down next to me and rests her head on my chest, but she's not as soft as before, or as warm. Yet she's still plenty warm and I've been so cold for a very long time.

"I get it now," she murmurs. "I get why you're the way you are."

I chuckle. "How am I?"

"Distant and cold, even though I know that's not the man you really are," she says. "But I get why now."

"No, you don't," I say, since she can't possibly, and it's a good thing she doesn't. "Go to sleep now. We've got a lot of riding ahead of us tomorrow."

She doesn't say anything else, since I guess even

she runs out of things to say eventually. It's better that way. She did find those few perfect things to say, but on the whole, there's nothing to say. Though I do feel less cold and hard having told her all that stuff and gotten it out of my head for a change. But I'm sure that won't last.

---

BARBIE

HE DOZED off soon after telling me his horrible life story, but I couldn't sleep. I suppose he had to get it off his chest, I could feel it weighing him down all this while, but I can't say I felt the weight lift after he told me either.

I was ready to fall asleep before he started talking, still floating on the last waves of the pleasure we shared, letting them lull me into a sweet dream, but I was wide awake again by the time he finished.

I remember watching him fight in the tournaments. Seven took me to a couple of fights, as did most of the guys I dated after him. I never liked going, and avoided it if I could, since I know exactly what it's like to get hit hard and find nothing enjoyable in it. For guys it's different, I guess. After Seven told me that lie about Ice, how he betrayed his club and helped slaughter them all, I liked going even less, since I couldn't understand why someone would do that. Or how someone *could* do that. Here I was, searching for a family I never really had and also never found, and this guy just sold his out and let them all be slaughtered? That never made any sense to me, even while I knew it for the fact I thought it was.

I believe him that it was all a lie. I saw the truth in his eyes when he spoke about his father and I doubt very much that a guy whose sister wanted him to play Barbie's with her, would just let her be killed a couple of years down the road. Everyone associated with his club was killed that night, I know that part of the story well. That's why the doctor at the hospital thought he was dead. She remembered him for the good guy he was — that he is— and that's why she believed him when he told her I didn't get my injuries from him. And he saved me, a complete stranger. No way a guy like that would help kill his entire family.

No, the way he told it makes perfect sense. Right down to the fact that he needed to kill all the Spawns in revenge. It's scary as fuck, and it frightened me hearing him talk about it, because I saw clearly that's all that mattered to him for a long time. But I get it. I also get why he thinks he can't give me a good time.

I'd still like him to try though, and I still think we can have a pretty damned good time on this trip. That might be because I'm fucked up in the head too, but I think we could make it work. I think me and him were meant to meet, that we're destined to be together, and to leave our brutal, bad pasts behind us together. Sleep came easy once I figured that out.

## 12

ICE

TODAY, I haven't been riding as hard or as fast as I did the last few days, haven't felt the need to. I've even been enjoying the scenery, the timelessness of the empty road, the freedom and peace it can offer.

When I was younger, before the Spawns destroyed everything, I'd take long rides just for the hell of it, just for the peace and quiet and calm. I've tried and tried to get back to that peace and calmness since I was freed, tried to make the echoes of it a reality again and again. But it never worked.

Not the time I went down to Mexico on my own, not on my ride out East to my hometown in Illinois.

There was never any peace on those rides and I needed some goal to keep going, like seeing my father's grave and the ruins of my childhood home. Before that, I needed a Spawn to kill at the end of the road, or to help Rook find that lady friend of his down in Mexico City, or getting Barbie to California, to keep my mind from wandering into the darkness I've spent so long alone in, and where I never get even a moment of peace from the hate, let alone any calm. That need was gone this morning and hasn't come back yet.

I forgot the world, how it smelled, how the road felt under the tires of my bike, how the light shimmers on the horizon on hot summer days, how creamy the clouds look. I forgot what freedom felt like long before I got it back. I even forgot I wanted it back. But I do now.

I also forgot how good a woman could feel and taste. I remember it clear as day now, Barbie reminded me, and I've been enjoying her warm and soft body pressed against my back. Very much so. I still say she should run away from me, but I'm starting to think it'd be nice, if she stayed for a little while longer anyway.

It's just past noon and the bright sun is reflecting off a body of water in the distance.

"Wanna stop at another lake?" I ask, since we're

going slow enough for her to hear me, which wasn't the case on our previous rides.

She smiles brightly at me through the rearview mirror, brighter than the sun. "Yeah, I do."

It's the least I can do, since I ruined our last trip to the lake. That was a good idea she had, to stop there, just the timing was off. But the timing feels pretty good right now, and we got plenty of time. I speed up so we can reach the lake faster.

"We should go for a swim," she says as she climbs off the bike once we do.

It's a hot day today, more summer than fall, and a bunch of people are already doing just that.

"The water's gonna be damn cold," I inform her.

She shrugs. "I'll take it. I haven't been swimming in years."

"Me either," I admit, and her eyes turn soft and sad. Pitying.

"I can't imagine being locked up for that long," she says, and I don't much like this additional reminder of what she's letting me forget. The pity in her eyes is already plenty. "I love to just go walking sometimes. Like for miles and miles. I can't imagine not being free to do that."

Her pity isn't as infuriating anymore after she tells me all that. But then again, I'm getting used to her saying exactly what needs to be said.

"I'm not in the mood for a hike right now," I tell her and grin, since I was never the best at knowing what to say and when. Maybe she really wanted to go for a walk, and I ruined it for her. But I was always good at speaking my mind, and I don't want to go walking. Right now, I want to watch her swim naked.

She grabs my hand, laces her fingers between mine and squeezes tight before she starts pulling me towards the water.

"That's fine," she says. "Because today I want to swim."

She lets go of my hand once we're almost at the lake and gives me a mischievous grin. "Stay right here."

Then she walks the few feet to the water's edge and stops near a family of five. She unzips her jacket, slides it off and tosses it on the ground by her feet. I only fully understand that she's stripping for me, once she pulls off her t-shirt slowly, twisting her body just so and making a show of it. She tosses the shirt at my chest then starts peeling off her skin-tight jeans equally slowly, ass towards me and out, a very large smile on her face as she looks over her shoulder at me. But it's probably not as big as the one on mine.

She's wearing a red bra and a red thong, and I

already saw both when she put them on this morning, but I could watch her all day. I have the urge to whistle at her, and I do it, which only works to alert the people who weren't already staring at us to turn their heads and gawk. But I don't care. She's a gorgeous woman and I want to be looking at her. And I want her to know just how much.

"Better leave the rest on, this seems like a family sorta place," I tell her as I join her by the water's edge. Not that I care. I don't really notice anyone else right now, not even the ghosts in my head. Just her.

"Let them look. They're all just jealous because we're free and we can do whatever we want," she says as she wraps her arms around my waist and kisses me.

Every time we do that, the ghosts retreat to some very far off place in my mind. And right now, that's even more pronounced, because they're gone. The kiss just lasts and lasts, my hard-on getting painful enough to forget we're not alone here. Or to not care that we aren't. Either way, it comes to the same thing. I want her and I need her, and that's all I care about. Hopefully the ghosts won't come back, and it'll stay that way for the rest of the day and the night too.

She slides my jacket off while we're still kissing,

unbuckles my belt right after and only stops to help me pull my t-shirt over my head.

There won't be much of my hard-on left after I get in the icy water that she starts leading me into, but that's alright, I'm sure she'll take care of that too.

The ocean would be better for this, but Cali's far off and it's not going anywhere. And this is a good day. Better than any I still remember clearly.

---

BARBIE

I WANTED him to take me right there in the water, even though it was so cold it took my breath away when I entered it, but that would've been too over the top. A lot of the people on the lakeshore removed themselves while we kissed and splashed around and did everything, but actually have sex. If we did that, someone would've called the cops and then we'd probably end up getting arrested, and be forced to spend the night apart, each in our own cell.

This is much better. We found a secluded spot under some trees right by the water and I'm leaning on him as he leans on a rock, his skin hot and soft against my back, his even breaths calming as I watch the sun descend towards the water in the distance.

I'm all soft inside from the last orgasm he gave me, sated and content. He's spent for now, his cock soft as it presses against the small of my back. I'll want more soon and I'll want it all over again after that, but this is nice too, very nice.

"You know, I don't remember the last time I felt this comfortable with a guy," I blurt out, and I wasn't exactly planning on voicing this particular thought right now, but it still feels good to tell him that.

He chuckles, the movement of his chest tickling my back. "Come on, Barbie, there's no need to feed me lines like that anymore. You got me for the time being."

He sounds like he really means all of what he just said. Both that I have him and that it's only for the time being. I bet his eyes are all wintery right now too, and am proven right as I look at him over my shoulder.

"I'm not just saying that," I tell him, because it's important for him to know "I mean it. And you should take that as a compliment, because I've been with a bunch of guys before you."

His eyes harden some more and even that grin on his face seems to be carved from ice now. "Yeah, we already established that. No need to keep reminding me."

"Alright, I won't," I say sheepishly, probably blushing a little, since, yeah, why the hell would I want to bring up the fact that I've slept around lots. Guys hate hearing that, they like to think the women they're with are all virgins.

I lean back against him, take his left hand in mine and start studying the lines on his palm. His love line is deep and even, but it starts later than mine, I notice as I compare them against each other.

"You reading my palm now?" he asks mockingly.

He doesn't take his hand away though.

"I've been thinking a lot about what that fortuneteller told me," I say, staring at my love line.

"She was just an old fraud who wanted your money," he says.

"Yeah maybe, but it's not what she said that I've been thinking about," I say and grin back at him. "It's this break in the love line on my palm. See, here?"

I show it to him, so he'll know what I'm talking about.

He takes my hand and peers at the spot I'm showing him, probably more to humor me than because he's taking this seriously, judging by the mocking half-smile on his face.

"I figured out what that gap means," I tell him

before he can say something mean. "And your palm confirms it."

"Oh, yeah? How's that?" he asks.

"I think we were meant to meet six years ago when I first came to your town, only you weren't there, because of what happened to you," I say, then pause to swallow hard, since I'm only just now realizing this is a very painful subject for him. But the point I'm trying to make is beautiful. I hope he'll see it that way too. "So it took that long for us to meet, but now we did. And your love line starts later, kinda at the same spot where mine takes up again. Don't you think?"

I open his palm to show it to him next to mine, and I'm kinda afraid to look back at him to see his reaction, but I gotta see it. Then I wish I hadn't looked, because that's not just winter in his eyes now, it's a blizzard.

"I think palm reading is a bunch of bullshit," he says in an ice cold voice.

I should've seen this coming, since most guys freeze up when love becomes the subject of a conversation, and this particular conversation must be painful for him in other ways too. I better take this down a notch, if I want to spend the night here in his arms and not the other way around, on the back of his bike with only my arms around him. And I really want that first option.

He's not yet ready to completely give into the rightness of him and me being together the way I am, but we've been progressing in leaps and bounds, and I'm sure he'll join me here soon.

"Yeah, maybe," I say, backtracking as I release his hand.

I shift and rub my butt against his cock, which begins to harden just from that little attention. "But going back to what you were saying before, I bet you were real popular with the ladies too, big boy. So don't even try to act all high and mighty with me."

He groans and grinds his cock into my ass, squeezing my breasts at the same time. He somehow always manages to pinch my nipples just so, making me give out a sharp "aaahhh" and forget what I was thinking.

"Oh, Barbie, where the hell did you come from?"

He doesn't even wait for an answer, probably because he's now afraid I'll start talking about love lines again. Instead he kisses my neck hungrily, hitting the exact right spot as he pinches my nipples just so again.

"I've always been right here, waiting for you," I say anyway, amid the moans and aahhhs his lips and his hands are coaxing out of me, because it's the truth as I see it.

He doesn't say anything to that, but his kisses, nips and bites get wilder, and amid all this undivided attention he's giving me, I grow even more certain I'm right. But soon, I can't think anymore.

I'm stroking his cock as I moan and writhe in his arms, and under his hands and fingers, which know exactly what to do with my body to give me the ecstasy every woman wants, but I've finally found.

It doesn't take long before the first sounds of the freight train of our lust and passion start hitting me. Before I know it, my knees and my palms are getting scraped up against the gravelly ground, his cock inside me, its thrusts opening up vast plains of pleasure that's beyond this world and the next. I feel no pain, only lust, only enjoyment, only the rightness, only the sense of belonging that only he can give me.

He goes so deep into me, yet there'll always be more room for him to take me out of this world and into another, one where all thinks sparkle and pleasure and laughter is possible all the time.

Before long, I can't even hold onto that thought anymore. His thrusts grow faster, go deeper still, and I'm writing and begging for a reprieve, even as I offer my pussy to him willingly, not moving away but pushing back to meet every one of his thrusts. I can't take this much good all at once, I'm not used to it. But then I get used to that too.

The setting sun is inside me now, making everything burn and shine, but not painfully, no, everything is just right, just perfect, just exactly the way I always wanted it to be. The river of my orgasm washes over it all, the light inside me reflecting off water, which can't douse the sparkling enjoyment, the bliss, the electric pleasure that only he can drown me in. And I him. Because I know that's a fact too, even if he doesn't yet.

---

ICE

SHE'S asleep in my arms and it's getting cold, but I don't want to move and put more wood on the fire, the few glowing embers of which are the only thing still fighting the pitch black night.

She talks a good game, this Barbie does. So good I almost believe her, almost believe that I could be the guy I was before for her. I do believe her when we kiss, or when I come inside her sweet little pussy, because at those times all that matters is how good she feels, and how good she makes me feel. Better than I thought I'd ever feel again.

But it all crashes once the passion is spent. Like right now, when she's asleep. That strip show she gave me by the lake took me right back to the time before Lizard, when life was all about having as much wild fun as I could cram into it, and I'll always be grateful to her for giving me that back even if just for an afternoon. Because even that's fading now too.

It's easier not to think about what could've been and wasn't, easier to stand being alive at all, while I listen to her speak. She has a pretty face and everything else on her is pretty too. Together with that good mouth on her and her good pussy, the whole package is weirdly perfect with her, I can't deny that. But I'm just her ride and she's just the girl I stole from someone else. And I'm just a guy who said goodbye to living and loving a long time ago.

Even as the last of the embers of our fire go out, the bad memories don't overshadow this great day we shared, the first in a year of days that were good but not in a good way. They were just good in a bloody, murderous, revengeful and angry way.

Even remembering all that, I still prefer to just fall asleep with her in my arms over anything else. For the first time in seven years, anger, hate and regret aren't the last thing on my mind as I start to doze off. Maybe they won't be the first thing on my mind when I wake up. But that's probably a stretch. She just tired me out today with her good mouth and her good pussy and her thirst for life, which I don't understand where she gets from.

---

No such luck on waking up feeling good. Seven's snarling face seconds before he died is burned over the image of Lizard holding his stomach, his black guts glistening in what little light came into the back of the van where I killed him. Even with my eyes wide open, I still see that part of my dream clearly. The sun's up, but it's not reaching the secluded, wooded area where Barbie and me spent the night. The fire is crackling and burning well, but she's gone. All her clothes are gone too. And I feel sick.

But before I even fully comprehend how all those things are connected and tied together, she comes charging up through the bushes, holding the white scarf that crazy palm reader gave her, and smiling brightly.

"Good, you're up," she says as she kneels on the ground next to me, and gives me a warm and sweet kiss.

I don't kiss her back, since I'm still trying to put everything floating around in my brain into some sort of coherent order. The last thing I was thinking before she showed up was that she's probably better off disappearing on me. And that made me angry, because it's not what I want.

She pulls back from the kiss and pouts at me. "What's wrong?"

I shrug, since I don't even know where to begin explaining any of that to her. But I do know her eyes are bright blue even in this grey half-light of a cold dawn, and that I really like looking into them.

"Did you think I left?" she asks, gasping a little but trying to hide it. "I just woke up real early and felt like taking a walk. It's been awhile since I've done that. I built you a nice big fire, so you wouldn't be cold while I was gone."

She points at the fire, but whatever she sees in my face makes her smile droop sadly.

I don't want her sad. I want to drink off this vibrancy she carries inside, which seems to have no end. So I don't waste any time, just pull her to me and kiss her like I should've done as soon as she showed up, because that's the only thing I really wanted to do, and it makes perfect sense even when nothing else does. Once she kisses me back and settles into my lap, the rest falls into its rightful place too, receding right to the back of my mind where it belongs now that it's all said and done.

The sun is much higher in the sky when we finally stop kissing, but that fire she built is still burning brightly.

"You make one hell of a camp fire," I tell her, smiling at her half closed eyes and glistening, swollen lips. "A better one than me."

She smiles too. "I was dirt poor growing up. No central heating, and no money to pay for it even if we had it. So it was either learn to build a good fire or freeze to death during the night. I learned to build a good fire."

"Yeah, you did," I say and brush a lock of her hair that's obscuring her eyes back behind her ear. I'm not just talking about an actual fire right now, I'm talking about the metaphorical one she lit for us too, for me, the one that's thawing up things inside me I thought were gone for good.

"Let's get some breakfast, babe," I tell her, smacking her ass lightly. "Unless you got good at hunting for food too, while you were growing up dirt poor, I mean. Then we can stay right here."

I laugh at the outrage on her face, and get smacked on the arm for it. "Hey, no need to poke fun at me."

"Yeah, I can't hunt worth shit either," I say and

grin, then kiss her again, because in a lot of ways, she's the only thing I'm hungry for right now.

———

BARBIE

HE WAS BROODING HARD when I returned from my walk, totally stopped while we were kissing, but he's kinda doing it again now as I push the last piece of my blueberry pancake around on my plate, because I'm absolutely too full to eat another bite.

"What's on your mind, big boy?" I ask, since I'm not gonna figure it out on my own and he's shown that he needs some prodding before he starts telling me stuff. And also that he feels better once he actually does tell me.

He shrugs and takes a long gulp of his coffee instead of answering. But I don't say anything, just wait for him to start talking. Sometimes it's better if I don't talk and with him, I'm learning very quickly when those times are.

"I've been doing some math in my head," he finally says, once he realizes I'm not gonna fill the silence with my yakking this time.

"Math's a waste of time," I interject into his pause,

since I can only get so far out of my chatterbox nature. "At least, I always thought so."

He grins, which is softer than the expression that was on his face before, but not by much.

"Well, this is the useful kind of math, the one that tells me we've been on the road long enough for that boyfriend of yours to recover and mobilize," he says and the mention of Brick makes me queasy. I wanna say he's not gonna come after me, but I know him too well. He's gonna try.

"He's probably already coming after us," he adds, echoing my thoughts.

"And good luck to him finding us," I say. "We're lost in the middle of nowhere. He's dumb and old, and he'll forget all about me soon enough. In fact, I bet he already has on that night we ran away together."

"What about that other guy?" Ice asks, grinning. "The one he was handing you off to?"

That one's trickier, and the thought of it makes me even more nauseous. "Razor's been after me for a long time, like stalking me and shit. But he's gotta give up eventually and this is a great time for him to finally learn that."

I laugh after I say it, but his face stays stone cold serious.

"He knows who I am and who I've been riding

with," he says and just by his tone alone, I know that this is the main reason why he's been brooding all through breakfast.

"I thought you had no one," I say, more quietly adding, "Like me."

His eyes grow a fraction softer. "I told you I had help getting my revenge on the Spawns. The guys from Devil's Nightmare MC helped me. They freed me and then they helped me kill them all."

The way he says that last makes the hair on the back of my neck stand up like I've been caught in a very cold breeze. But maybe that's also because he mentioned the Devils. I've heard of them, everyone has, and no one likes to say much about them, one way or the other. But everyone knows that they're stone cold killers who'll murder anyone if the price is right.

"Brick will never go against the Devils," I say. "He's too scared of them. And I'll bet Razor is too."

He grins, doubt clear in his eyes. "You heard of the Devils? Or did you just date a couple of them too?"

I shake my head and I don't like his insinuation, so I'm gonna ignore it. "Everyone's heard of the Devils. Stories about them are like children's scary stories for adult bikers. Brick won't go to them looking for me."

He barks a laugh. "They're not that bad. My sister is their president's old lady, and she's having his baby. I'd rather not risk any of their lives on the assumption that Brick and Razor are a couple of cowards."

"Your sister is alive? I thought she was dead too," I say way too brightly and excitedly for what I'm actually saying, but right now I'm just really happy that it's so.

He nods, but the expression on his face is far from happy. "I caught up to Lizard and the rest of his scum just in time to save her on that night when they murdered everyone else. He was gonna keep her alive and do things I'd rather not think about to her, but I stopped it. I was gonna kill him that night, or die trying, but instead I prevented him from taking her and let myself get taken instead."

I'm getting teary-eyed listening to him and I practically never get teary-eyed over anything. The last time I cried was when I lost my baby. I grab his hand in both of mine and squeeze reassuringly. He doesn't pull it from my grasp, but it's dead weight in mine.

"Nothing will happen to your sister, she's safe," I say. "We won't go there and that's that. Even Brick and Razor won't demand the return of someone who's not there to be given back. They're dumb, but not that dumb."

The half smile he gives me suggests I'm the dumb one. "Men retaliate for all sorts of reasons, big or small. What Lizard did to my father and our MC, that was over nothing at all, a dumb turf dispute that shouldn't have escalated into a war, but it did. For years, I believed my sister was dead, because Lizard lied to me and told me he found her and had killed her. I believed that right up until the moment the Devils' president told me he freed me for her. I don't wanna mourn her again. I don't wanna mourn any of them."

He's not calling me dumb, I was wrong about that. He's apologizing. Apologizing to me, because he thinks he can't save me from Brick and Razor. And he's sad because he'll have to let them have me, if they find us. I don't know much, and I'm a simple girl, but I know all that, and I know I'll never let him just hand me over to someone else without a fight. Because I know we're meant to be together.

I get up without letting go of his hand and walk over to his side of the booth. "Scooch over."

He looks at me questioningly, but does it. And all those things I know make even better sense once I lean in real close to him and only let go of his hand so I can wrap my arms around his waist. "We're in this together, Ice. I'm not going back to Brick, and I know you don't want that either. So we're just gonna have to figure it out."

"That's kinda always been your plan, Barbie, hasn't it?" he asks. "Just go with the flow, come what comes?"

I nod and smile at him. "Yes, and now you came. And that's all I ever wanted. I'm not letting you go."

He shakes his head even as he wraps his arm around my shoulders and hugs me tightly. "Life's not that simple."

"Yeah, it is. It's as simple as you and me right here," I say and kiss his cheek. "Besides, you didn't steal me from Brick. You fought them for me and they lost. Even dumb bastards like them understand something like that. Brick didn't want me anymore anyway, and him and Razor were never very good friends. I doubt we'll ever see either of them again. Especially not if it means messing with the Devils."

That might be a bit of a stretch, but it makes sense too.

"I hope you're right," he says and kisses the top of my head, the last of the tension finally leaving his body. It was always there in the beginning, gone for the last day or so, came back while he was talking about his fears, but now it's gone again and it better never return.

"Hope's really all that matters. It's what gets you out of bed in the mornings," I say.

"Yeah, but wanting to kill someone in revenge works just as well," he says, all cold and tense again. This is something he knows and I don't, so a good reply escapes me.

He's not waiting for one though. He just leans down and kisses me, his hand slipping under my t-shirt, squeezing my belly as his tongue invades my mouth. And I forget trying to find something to say, forget the cold stab to the heart his words felt like, forget everything but my sparkling, glowing hope that we will figure this out.

"Hope is better," I mutter, the reply miraculously appearing once his lips leave mine.

He grins. "Yeah, you're probably right."

He kisses me again and after awhile of that, I'm sure we don't even need to hope for anything, because all we've ever wished for is already ours.

## 13

BARBIE

WE SPENT the last few days just cruising under the sun that's getting warmer with each mile we cover, and making love, and falling asleep in each other's arms under the stars on nights that keep getting warmer too, the closer we get to the ocean. All of it has run together into just one endless day in my mind, eternal and never ending. In other words, this is better than any road trip I used to daydream about taking. The rest of my daydreams are coming true too, so hard and so fast, I have no need for them anymore. They have become my reality.

Warm wind is brushing my bare arms now as we

ride, and the world around us is bathed in the soft brownish hues of a hot summer afternoon. The air shimmers on the horizon and there's no one but us on this perfectly straight road for as far as I can see. It's been that way for the whole day. We're alone in this world, just the two of us amid all this wild beauty stretching out towards eternity before us and behind us, and off to both sides of the road too. I wouldn't want it any other way. Well, maybe I'd prefer to be lying with him in a field of grass, naked, satisfied and happy, but only just.

I can make at least a part of that daydream a reality right now. I'm holding onto him tight, tighter than I need to because we aren't going fast. His t-shirt is flapping in the wind, his smell mixing with all the other scents of late summer on the air, of the open road and freedom. I slide my hand under his t-shirt.

His scent and the feel of his strong body in my arms will forever be tied in my mind with freedom and belonging, with the gorgeous sights only the open road can offer, of clear untouched waters, of green lush forests and the empty, straight roads, of the tall grasses and trees swaying in the fields lining them that sometimes stretch out as far as my eyes can see, of clouds gathering on the horizon with rays of sunshine piercing them, all of it so close to the ground it's like the heavens are touching the earth, of the fresh scent of dawn in the middle of nowhere. It will forever be tied to the kind of oneness I've never felt before and probably never will again.

His body feels even better than I imagined it would too. The rippling valleys and peaks of his abs and his chest are all I can touch at the moment, but I'll get my chance at the rest too. Soon, I hope.

"Keep going," he says and grins at me in the rear view mirror as he loosens his belt, leaving me with no doubt as to what he's suggesting. That's just how it is between us, we don't even have to speak much— most of the time we don't even have to speak at all— to be understood by each other. And that's a huge part of why I have no need for daydreams anymore.

I grin back and keep caressing his abs like I've been doing. "I just wanted to feel your skin."

He shrugs and grins wider. "Fair enough, I like your skin a lot too."

And that's no lie, he likes to kiss and lick every inch of my skin, so this is just a plain statement of fact, and one of the nicest compliments I've ever gotten. Because it came from his heart.

After awhile, the road we're riding on fills up and comes up real close to an interstate. A fair sized town is visible in the distance, the first one we've passed close to in days.

"Let's stop and go dancing tonight," I say into his ear. "And I kinda want to sleep in a real bed too."

I kiss his neck without waiting for a reply, because it's right there and he smells so nice and he feels so good in my arms, and I want all of him all the time.

"Alright, Barbie, let's do it." The way he says it kinda makes me think he'd give me anything I asked for, and that feels amazing too.

I've known for awhile now that I'd give him anything he asked me for. I should tell him that, but I've been waiting for the right moment.

---

WE ENDED up in a bar that's also a restaurant to kill two birds with one stone, as he put it—get some food and take me dancing at the same time. We've finished dinner about an hour ago and the place is starting to fill up with the evening crowd coming here for a good time, since apparently it's Saturday night. I'd lost all track of time awhile back, and even now, knowing it, the day of the week has no meaning. We haven't found a place to sleep yet, which is a good thing, since we'd probably just stay in, if we'd done that first, but not to sleep. That would've been fun too, but so's this, and I want it to last.

We're not even talking, we're just holding hands, looking at each other and smiling. Even though the place is pretty full, I feel like we're still alone, out on the open road, just him and me getting lost under the sun, everything inside me vibrating to the tune of his bike. Everything inside me is still vibrating, and I think that's because he's the source of it and not his bike, so it'll never go away. I hope it doesn't, because I love it.

"You're not dancing," he remarks, grinning at me.

Some country song is playing on the radio, but it's not very loud and not very danceable to. I've been eying the jukebox in the corner for awhile now to fix that.

"Do you think that thing works?" I ask, pointing at it.

He looks at it, then reaches into his pocket and tosses some change on the table. "Why don't you go check it out? I wouldn't mind seeing you dance."

"Oh, you like dancers, do you? Well, then you're in for a treat." I give him a coy grin then scoop the money off the table and sway my hips over to the jukebox, feeling his eyes on me even after I can't see them anymore.

I'm wearing the black beach dress I got when I went shopping on that first day in preparation for going to the beach. It's tight, has a low neckline and even though it's a maxi dress, it has slits on both sides that come almost up to my hips. He's not the only guy watching me as I walk across the bar, but I feel his gaze most of all.

The jukebox looks new and fully operational, but there's hundreds of songs to choose from, and I can't think of the perfect one. The longer I stare at it, the harder it is to decide. What's the one song that would make this evening even more perfect?

I feel him standing right behind me a split second before he envelops me with his arms and presses his strong body against my back. He didn't startle me, not even a little bit, because I'll always know him, even with my eyes closed, even if I were blind.

"What's taking so long?" he asks.

Then he kisses my neck and makes it impossible to answer, makes my pussy tingle and grow wet for him. By the time he pulls away, I'm pretty ready to scratch the whole dancing idea and go straight to bed.

"I can't pick," I complain, leaning against him and swaying a little. I don't need a special song to dance for him, the one playing in my heart since I met him is enough.

"How about this one?" he says and points to some hard rock tune that's completely wrong for what I had in mind.

"That was playing when I got you away from those assholes," he adds just as I'm about to tell him so. It kinda takes my breath, both because he remembered a thing like that, but also because he's wrong. I'm also pissed at myself for not thinking to play the song that was playing the night when we found each other.

"No, it was this one," I point to another song, a ballad that I clearly remember hearing the chorus of as we escaped through the back door. I could still hear it playing as Brick followed us outside and Ice beat him up.

"No, it was definitely this one," he says. "I remember it was pissing me off, because it was so loud I couldn't hear what you were talking about before I came over. The other one started later."

I crane my neck to look at him. That winter that was always in his eyes before is pure spring now, blooming gorgeous and just for me. "I guess they're both our song then. Which one should I play?"

He smiles. "Which ever you want."

I'm a simple woman and hearing things like that melts my heart. Or maybe that's only happening, because he's the first guy I truly believe means those words when he says them to me.

"OK, well, I'll play the one we can dance to," I say and press play on the ballad.

He twirls me around and keeps holding me, and we're not really dancing, just holding each other as we lock eyes and sway to the music. We're still just doing that long after our song finishes playing. I didn't hear a single note of it anyway, I didn't have to for this to be more perfect than any daydream I could come up with.

"Let's get out of here," he suggests later, when the dance floor is already packed with other couples and it's getting loud. I feel drunk although I never even finished that second beer we ordered. Drunk and giddy and so happy to be alive, happier than I've ever been to be alive.

"Yes, let's," I say and take hold of his hand as we walk out, because I'm not yet ready to stop holding him.

It's chilly outside and we've got a long way back to our bike, which we left near the edge of the downtown area to go in search of a nice place to eat and dance. But I don't need a jacket, his arm around my shoulders is enough to keep me warm even against the coldest wind. He's not wearing a jacket either, or he'd probably offer it to me, and knowing that makes it all just that much more perfect.

"Hey, I know," I say, pulling him to a stop in front of a tattoo place with a bright red neon sign announcing it. "We could get you a new tattoo. Actually, we could get matching ones."

He eyes the place skeptically then narrows his eyes at me. "You have a thing for getting matching tattoos, don't you?"

He's not being mean, I can tell that from his eyes and the sound of his voice, but I don't actually understand what he meant.

"Not especially," I say slowly. "But with you it'd be different."

I finish it with a bright smile, which should leave him with no doubt as to what I really mean.

"Not especially?" he asks then pulls my hand up so it's under the light. "And the guy who has the other half of this, what's he? A puff of smoke?"

He's pointing at the half a heart I have tattooed on the outside of my left palm.

"A puff of smoke? That's funny and pretty accurate too," I say and smile up at him, because this night just got a little more perfect.

"I got this a long time ago. And I got it by myself, thinking that once I find the right guy, the perfect guy, he could get the other half on his right hand. Like this…" I press my palm against his, lacing our fingers together, and point to the empty spot on his that's level with my half heart. "If you had the other half then we'd make a whole heart together. I thought that'd be so cool, but it's been ten years or more since I started looking. But now...well...you could get the other half tonight, if you want."

I should've found a better way to ask him that, but it'd be so perfect, I couldn't waste any time thinking of the right words. I just had to say it.

His face tightens, his eyes get wide and he looks very frozen for the split second before he laughs. "Funny joke there, Barbie."

"I meant it," I protest, not sure how this conversation veered off track so spectacularly fast. A split second ago the whole world seemed to be spinning towards finally saying those three little words to each other that I've been dying to say and hear for days. I was gearing up to tell him how I truly feel about him, that I love him, and I expected to hear it back.

"Sure you did," he says lazily like he's taking none of it seriously, but that look in his eyes is plenty serious, so I truly don't know what's what anymore.

"Let's go in and you can get those butterflies around your kid's name," he says. "And I'll get a butterfly too, so I'll have something to always remember you by."

He's already holding the door open for me so I go inside, even though I'd rather protest this turn of events and ask why he'll need to remember me when I plan to be with him all the time from now on.

Before I know it, we're sitting side by side in the chairs. He's getting a butterfly that looks a lot like the one on my back put on permanently on his arm, and I'm getting four tiny versions of it around the date on my arm. It's something I've wanted for a long time, but never had the courage to go in by myself and ask for it, because I knew I'd just end up crying for days afterwards and tears are pointless. They're staying put in my throat now as the guy starts piercing my skin, and I know I'd never have the strength to sit here and let it happen if Ice wasn't right beside me holding my hand. But a tear does trickle down my face once the first butterfly is complete.

Now my baby will finally be able to fly free and happy. Because that's what butterflies are. They form in an ugly, hard cocoon into something so beautiful, so perfect, so light and free and alive there's nothing else like it in the world. That's what my baby would've been, one of a kind, perfect, special and more besides. Now I can finally let him go, let him be a butterfly in a better place. And for the first time in years, I feel like I can be and have all those things too. Because Ice is holding my hand.

———————

ICE

SHE'S SLEEPING, but I'm wide awake, sweating and my heart pounding from another nightmare that was bad enough to wake me. I've had nightmares almost every night since I got captured by Lizard, and they didn't stop after I was freed. If anything, they're getting worse now that I stopped thinking about all the things wrong with my life, my mind, my future and my past during the day. I stopped doing that once I let Barbie talk me into enjoying this road trip her way, though I didn't need much convincing. She's the best lay I've ever had, and she's a lot of fun spending time with when fully clothed too.

But I'm forgetting that as I fight this losing fight with pushing down the nightmare. It took me right back to that night, to the moment I returned to the clubhouse after getting a hurried, barely coherent phone call that everything and everyone was going to hell. It was all as vivid and realistic as when it happened, more like a memory than a dream. I've never seen so many people dead in one place, not before nor since. The clubhouse was already burning when I reached it, but I could see the bodies clearly through the windows. They didn't have a chance, they were all killed before the place was set alight. In real life, I went to my father's house next. I found it engulfed in flames, but saw the red lights of bikes in the distance at the very end of the road leading past my childhood home and out of town. I took off after the lights, not knowing what I'd find when I reached them, but hoping it'd be Lizard so I could kill him. I found Lizard and I found my sister. I saved her, but I didn't kill him.

However, this time the nightmare took me to Sanctuary after showing me the burning clubhouse and dead bodies, to the place my sister now calls home and it was burning too. She was dead, her whole family was dead, and fire was destroying everything my six years of being treated worse than a fighter dog bought. I couldn't stand knowing it, so I woke up. But now I still can't stop seeing it.

Barbie was the cause of all that destruction. Or I was, for stepping in because I couldn't watch her get beaten. But in real life, she's also the cause of me being able to forget all the nightmares—the real ones, and the ones I dream—for hours, for days at a time.

She came within an inch of telling me she loved me last night, because that's what she thinks is happening. Good thing I averted it, else we'd have a problem on our hands right now. I can't love. I don't even love my sister anymore, she was dead to me for too long. *I* was dead to me for too long, and I'm not coming back to life.

But I'll enjoy the butterfly on my arm, enjoy the memories of Barbie and how good she felt in my arms and on my dick and lying next to me. And of how easily she made me forget the bad for hours at a time. But there's no forgetting forever. This empty dead weight of regret and hate in the pit of my stomach as I try to disregard the nightmare is proof enough of that.

I haven't been in touch with Roxie or Cross since I met Barbie, but we're gonna reach Nevada today and California the day after. I'll call them later today to see what's happening. I hope nothing, but while hope is a very nice thing to have—Barbie showed me that too—it's just a puff of smoke, easily swallowed up and destroyed by the reality that I stole her from two guys who are gonna want her back, and will probably shed blood to get her. In my experience that kinda thing is a matter of principal with old-timers like that, more often than not.

I won't let them have her, and that means I can't have her either. But I'm gonna enjoy Barbie some more before we get to that crossroads.

She's a sweet girl, a sensitive, but strong girl with a bad past, and she's got lots of love to give. She should give it to someone who can give it back to her, because that's what she wants and it's what she deserves. But it's not something I can give her.

She hasn't seen any of my demons, not since that first night I fucked her, and that's because she makes me forget so well. They're always there though, right below the surface, waiting, growling, and sharpening their claws. I don't want her to meet them.

Her skin always tastes like she just got caught in a spring shower, and she smells better than all the flowers of spring combined. She moans in her sleep while I kiss her neck and her breasts and her belly, but doesn't wake up until I find her nipples, which are always erect and ready for action. Playing with them never once fails to pull that sweet little sound of enjoyment-slash-surprise from her throat, and it's the same now.

Her neck tastes best of all, and her moans are the sweetest while I'm kissing it. I love how her racing heartbeat and this soft purring sound she's making tickle my lips. I love the feel of her palms gliding across the back of my head and my neck, my shoulders, my arms, and my chest, as she surrenders her softest parts to me like I'm not a monster. But the thing is, she just hasn't met the monster yet, because she's been so good at keeping it away.

Her pussy is warm and soft and always wet, and I love how it tastes too. She has the nicest, most sensitive clit, prettier than any flower, and she comes so fast when I play with it. Like right now, she's already on the very edge, purring and moaning and playing with her nipples while I lick and bite and get my fill of the taste of her. But I won't let her come yet. Right now, we're gonna go slow.

She can't hide the disappointment as I stop playing with her pussy and kiss my way back up to her neck. I guide her onto her side, and her purring moan rises in pitch and intensity as I rub my cock over her pussy. I can't help but moan a little too, since there's nothing quite like the feel of her velvet soft clit against my rock hard cock. So I do that for some time, while kissing her neck and letting her purring moans cause ripples in my blood. But being inside her is even better than this.

She inhales sharply once I give her my cock. I'm entering her pussy slowly and deliberately, half inch by half inch. Her moan doesn't end, just keeps getting deeper and louder, audible even as I kiss her lips and she kisses me back. I'm holding her tight, kissing her well, my cock now buried all the way inside her sweet, wet pussy. If I could give her even more of me, I would. But this is it. This is all I have to give her.

I pull out slowly then give it all to her again. She comes before I fully enter her the second time, her whole body rigid, her pussy gripping my cock tight like she's never gonna let go, and her moan stuck silent in her throat.

I'm not done yet, not even close, and she'll take more, because she loves to come, and I love watching her come. She opens like a flower when she does, all traces of that smart-ass, slutty exterior of hers parting to reveal the full extent of how beautiful she really is. She's beautiful through and through, and she's too beautiful for me. Too beautiful for anyone I know. But she chose this life and that was her mistake.

Pretty soon the long strokes I'm giving her start working their magic on me too. All else is fading, falling away, and nothing but how good she feels, and how gorgeous and pure she is, matters. Absolutely nothing. I pick up the pace, making her moan and purr louder. We come at the same time, her pussy gripping my cock and her fingers like a vise on my arm. She takes all I have to give her and doesn't ask for anything more. It's completely dark in the room, but the sun is shining too, and it's her.

I don't let go of her once we're spent, don't take

my cock out as I doze off, because I want this to last for as long as it can.

My reasons are different from the ones stopping her from getting off my cock and extricating herself from my embrace. Hers are loving, mine are selfish. I want to sleep the rest of this night without night-mares, and I think being this close to her will work. But she deserves better than that.

14

_____

ICE

WE NOT ONLY REACHED NEVADA, we've now nearly
crossed it, because I've been in no mood for just
cruising today. I didn't have another nightmare last
night, but the one her softness and her purring
moans chased away lingered. Which is a shame,
because Nevada is one good looking state to ride
through, if you have the time and the peace in your
head. I have neither. The sun's starting to set, it's still
hot as hell, and I've been putting off this phone call
long enough.

   There might be no news. Barbie and I might be
free to do some more riding before the reckoning

comes. But I gotta know. That damn nightmare's been flashing before my eyes all day, and nothing Barbie does or says is chasing it away.

She's sitting there all pretty on my bike, with one of her long, tasty legs propped up on the seat and nothing but soft brown desert all around her. This gas station I pulled into looks closed, but the payphone works. Nothing's moving in this heat except the air around Barbie, that's all wavy and shimmering like she's the source of it.

"Ice, where the hell have you been?" Roxie asks in that shrill voice she gets when she's worried and which always annoyed me no end. As it does now, especially since I can sense there's more to it than a mere annoyance that I haven't called her in a couple of weeks. Or maybe that's just my fear talking.

"Riding," I tell her. "How's everything there?"

She doesn't answer and I can hear her speaking to someone.

"I'm good, and the baby's good too," she says as she comes back on the line. "Cross wants to talk to you."

Here comes the reckoning.

"Put him on," I tell her, my voice all tight. But not as tight as my chest. I've caused so much shit for this guy already, and he's not even my president. He has every right to tell me to go to hell right now.

Seconds tick by and he doesn't come on the line. I can hear rusting and footsteps then a door rattling shut. He's probably in that posh office of his now, because he doesn't want Roxie to hear what he's about to tell me. Though knowing my sister, she'll probably ferret it out of him later anyway.

"What have you been up to, Ice?" he asks, uncharacteristically not getting to the point right away.

"This and that," I tell him, but don't go on, since I have no idea where to begin telling him about what's happening.

"I've been getting calls about a certain woman you took without permission," he says once he gets tired of waiting for me to speak. "They want her back."

"Without permission? Since when do I need permission to hook up with a woman? That guy was just giving her away to some other dude, and she didn't want to go. So I helped her out. And girl-friends aren't something you gift, they're not things. Or are they?" I wanted to start this conversation differently, but damn it if this isn't important either.

"Be careful what you say, Cross. You're with my sister," I add when he doesn't answer right away, kinda regretting it once it's out there, but kinda not.

I understand perfectly well that rules about club whores and old ladies are different for every club.

My father had strict but fair ones, and no one dared mess with any of our ladies, not even the brothers. But I don't exactly know what Cross' rules are, although the women I've seen at their clubhouse were treated well and seemed happy to be there.

"Don't worry about Roxie," he says, chuckling softly. "I take good care of her. She's happy and well-looked after."

Nothing I've seen or heard suggests otherwise. I shouldn't have brought this up.

"Let me start this conversation again," he says. "The Bloods and the Kings claim you disrespected them by taking a woman that belongs to them. They want her back, and they're coming here to get her."

The world stops and grows even hotter as I hear that, but it's what I expected to hear, I just hoped I wouldn't. So much for hope. Revenge always trumps it. I hoped Barbie wouldn't have to learn that lesson as clearly as I have, but here it is.

"I'm not giving her back to them," I say.

Cross sighs. "I didn't expect you to. Bring her here, and we'll figure it out. But I will avoid blood-shed, I'm telling you that right now. If she's some president's old lady and they didn't say goodbye properly, then they're gonna have to do that, one way or another. I'm not getting us into the middle of another war."

"When are they due?" I ask, ignoring all the other things he said, along with the tightness in my chest, which is already turning into cramps.

"I didn't do much talking to the guy who called. Told him that you're not here and she's not here. Hawk is keeping a lookout for them though," Cross says. "Either way, you should come here."

"It's better if I stay away," I say. "Then you can just keep telling them you know nothing about me."

"No, Ice, that's not how it works," he says. "We'll help you make this right."

"You've done enough for me, Cross," I tell him, since it's the truth. "I won't bring this down on you. I've done enough of that kinda thing already."

"Like I said, not how it works. You won't call yourself our brother, and I get why, but we all consider you one," he says, speaking slowly like he's explaining all this to a child. I don't like this turn in the conversation, it makes the regret and hate in my stomach an even heavier empty, dead weight.

"If you want to keep this woman, we'll help you out," he adds with a chuckle. "But we'll do it peacefully, is what I'm saying."

And yeah, I guess that's what he's been saying all along.

The air around Barbie is still shimmering, but

that just makes her look more like a dream now, like a mirage, something that's not really there.

"I won't risk any more brothers," I say quietly, not even sure if I said it aloud or not.

"Come home, Ice. Roxie wants to see you, and I know she wants to meet this new lady friend of yours. Then we'll figure all this out," he says.

What he's saying makes perfect sense. But I know how little it takes for lives to be lost. The thing that ended my father's life, and all my brothers' lives was so tiny, no one had ever heard of a war breaking out over it. But they all died anyway.

I tell him sure, even though I'm not thrilled about lying to him, but I see no other way out of this conversation at the moment. Roxie might want to see me, but she knows what's at stake as well as I do, and she'll get over not seeing me once I explain.

But I'm not gonna do that right now.

What I'm gonna do now is enjoy Barbie some more, while I still have her.

---

BARBIE

EVERYTHING IS PERFECTLY STILL, not even a breeze

stirring this suffocating, hot air, but for some reason I feel things breaking, shattering and crumbling before my eyes as I watch him talk on the phone. He's glancing at me every so often, but it's like he doesn't even see me, like I'm just a ghost, and that thought gives me the shivers despite the heat. I don't have to know much to know that we're getting close to the ocean. This is Nevada and California is next. I know that much. I also know that I don't want our trip to end yet.

"You know, I was thinking," I say as he approaches. "After we reach the ocean we could just keep going."

The shadows on his face have no place being there, because it's a bright sunny day.

"Keep going where?" he asks harshly. "It's the ocean, there's nothing forward of it except more water."

I stand up and wrap my arms around his waist, but he doesn't hug me back, he just stands there like a slab of stone.

"I know how the ocean works," I chide. "I meant, we could turn back once we reach it, maybe go down south or something. You know, just keep riding."

His eyes are frosty enough to give me the chills despite the heat all over again. The winter is back in them, and it's a bad one. They're saying, "No", loud and clear, but he's not actually saying it, and that's something. I guess. I hope.

"Let's get some dinner and a drink," he says and moves away from me just as I was about to kiss him, because that's the one thing that always makes everything alright.

I nod and let him go, get on the bike and don't say anything more, but I feel the pressure mounting. Something went wrong during that call he made. No, something's been wrong since we left the motel at dawn, despite the sweet way he made love to me in the middle of the night and how tightly he held me until morning. That's why he's been riding so fast all day.

All my failed relationships are playing on repeat in my mind, and I hope this isn't the beginning of the end for us. But I've seen plenty of ends, and this feels like one of them, no matter how hard I hope I'm wrong. Even holding on tight and leaning against his back doesn't help. And that scares me.

"Is everything alright with your sister," I ask once we're sitting at a roadside restaurant on the edge of another town that's bigger than the last one we stopped at.

This time, there was no parking on the edge of it to go in search of a cool place to eat. He just pulled into the first place we passed and here we are. Eating and not talking. Well, I'm talking, but it's a one sided conversation, and it doesn't look like that's about to change.

The sun is setting lilac and purple outside the window, and I wish I was enjoying it with his arms around me, but he's taking up the entire bench on his side of the booth, and I don't think he wants any company. For the first time since we met, I'm kinda reluctant to keep pushing myself on him. This is just like those first few days we spent together, only so much worse because those days weren't supposed to return, we left them far behind. I thought.

"Yeah, she's fine," he says and eats the last bite of his steak.

"You can finish the rest of mine, if you want," I say and push my plate towards him. I barely touched my food. "But me, I could go for another beer. Then we could play a game of pinball."

I've been eyeing the pinball machine in the corner since we got here, thinking how nice it'd be to play it with his arms wrapped around me. Free and carefree, the way it used to be. It's been so long since I did something like that with a guy I loved that the memory of it is faded like an old photograph. Then maybe we could dance some, like we did the other night. That'd be nice too.

He shakes his head, and stops the advance of my plate across the table. "Get a beer if you want, but then I just wanna get out of here and find a place to sleep."

My pussy pings at the thought that we'll probably not do much sleeping, but I'm sure he wasn't actually suggesting a night of passion. He looks tired and weary, and sounds like the only thing he wants to do is sleep. But then he grins as I smile, so maybe I'm wrong.

"I'll skip the beer. We can just go to bed," I suggest, and I do like that sparkle in his eyes, but the winter's still blizzarding in there, everything frozen. I see the same cold edge in his eyes that I saw the first night he took me. It's faint, but it's there, and I don't know what that means. He's been nothing but good to me since we met. Please don't let that change tonight.

I don't say anything more while he pays, then follow him out and get on the back of the bike, and just nod when he points out a motel and asks for my opinion.

"Well, this place looked better on the outside," I

remark, as we enter the room, which smells like a lemony cleaner that doesn't quite mask the stench of old and dirty things underneath it.

He pulls me to him and grinds his cock into my belly. "Do you really care?"

I don't like his tone, it's too much like when he called me a whore in the beginning and not like the way he's been talking to me since. But his kiss is sweet and full of hope and promise for better things, and once it gets going, I no longer know what to think, or how to.

But something started changing inside him and between us, when I asked him to get that half a heart tattoo to match mine, started boiling while he was on the phone with his sister, and it's spilling over hot and scathing now. And not in a good way. I feel that freight train approaching, the ground is shaking beneath my feet because it's going so damn fast, and this time it will run me over. It will kill me. I know it will and that pisses me off.

I wish he'd just tell me what's bothering him. Then we could figure it out together. Because him figuring it out on his own is just leading him back to that cold wintery place that I had such a hard time dragging him out of in the first place.

He's already ripping my dress off, one of its cheaply made straps tearing, which pisses me off even more, because I was supposed to wear it to the beach. The beach he promised to take me to, but I'm no longer sure that's where we're heading anymore.

"Easy there," I snap, as he squeezes my boob too hard, while biting down on my neck too hard at the same time. That was just pain, no pleasure. And it's like he's not even here with me.

He responds by kissing me wildly and tugging on my dress some more, but I want to salvage what I can of it. Maybe I can still sew the strap back on, but that won't work if he just rips the whole thing to shreds.

"Let me get that for you," I say and smile at him as I try to take a step back. There's no fire in his eyes, no softness, no loving spring, only ice. But I know he has all those things and plenty of them for me, so where are they hiding?

For a second I fear he's not gonna let me go, but he does, and I turn my back on him, let him get a good look at my ass as I peel the dress down to my ankles.

"You like looking at my ass, don't you, big boy?" I ask, trying to make this fun again.

His eyes and his face are incredibly hard though, too hard. I don't like it. He doesn't want to have fun. Why the hell am I even trying? Inside, I'm desperate and nervous like I get every time I feel an end approaching with a guy. But this time I'm angry too, because we're meant for each other. There can't be an end for us. I think it's staring me right in the face regardless.

"My personal theory is that the more a guy likes ass, the more of a dog he is," I tell him, because I can't hold my angry disappointment in anymore. The winter in his eyes turns to a frozen wasteland that's even scarier than the winter was. I went too far and I didn't mean it. He's not one of those guys. He's the best guy I ever met.

But something snapped inside him when I said it, and I know how badly before he even closes the distance between us and wraps his arm around me. Not gently like he did by the jukebox.

"You calling me a dog?" he growls more than says. "That's funny, I was just thinking about how much fun it'd be to fuck your ass for a change."

He's already undoing his belt and my heart is racing. "No, Ice, come on, not just like that."

But he's not listening as he forces me forward towards the bed.

"I wasn't calling you a dog. I shouldn't have said that."

He's still not listening and he already has me on my stomach on the bed.

The bed shakes and groans as he kneels over me,

holding me down with one of his strong hands on my upper back. With the other, he's already pulling my thong string aside. I can't get away, I can't even move very well.

I hear him spit into his palm, his hard cock hot and pulsing against my ass cheek.

"I can't take you like that," I complain.

"You'll do just fine, a girl like you," he says.

He's probably not wrong. I've taken it that way many times, and I even like it when done right. But he's so huge, and I feel no love inside of him right now.

"Let me turn around, Ice," I say. "Let's kiss some more first."

I'm trying to turn on my own, but he's not letting me. And I can't even relax, because this is too wrong, too harsh, too much like everything I hoped he wouldn't be. Things are well and truly breaking right now, crumbling to dust in my mind and all around me. And it hurts so bad.

Any moment now he's gonna thrust that huge cock of his into my ass, and I'll have no choice but to take that pain too. But moments float by and he doesn't. I'll just have to relax and take it, like I've had to so many times before, but hoped I wouldn't with him, because he always said things like, "Whatever you want, Barbie", and "If you'd like", but he never said those other three important words. He never said them because he doesn't love me. He's not the guy I thought he was. He's not my only one, not my soul mate. I was wrong. And I'm already crying, even though I never cry.

Any moment now, he's gonna show me just how wrong I was, because I wouldn't take his word for it. I don't know what's taking him so long now. He's still holding me down, his cock is still rock hard and pulsing hot against my asshole, but he's not thrusting it in. This could feel so good if he'd go slow, if he'd let me get used to it first, if he'd done it out of love. But he's not gonna do it out of love tonight, because he doesn't love me. The pain in my mind is bad enough, and I can't even take the thought of him physically hurting me, let alone this drawn out anticipation of it.

"Please, Ice, you're hurting me too much," I sob, giving it one last shot to turn tonight around.

He grows heavier on top of me, but then he just lets me go, removing all the weight as he stands up. It leaves me light headed, because I didn't expect it. I expected him to fuck my ass regardless of my pleas, because that's how it always goes. Most guys enjoy hurting me even more if I beg them to stop.

Yet he did stop, he didn't rape me, he didn't hurt me physically. But he almost did. The next time he might, and I promised myself I'd leave him the second he hurt me. But that was before I fell hopelessly in love with him. How can I leave him now? Why doesn't he love me back?

By the time I get my sobbing and my racing thoughts under control enough to turn around he's already opening the door.

"I did warn you about me, Barbie," he says and doesn't meet my eyes. "You should've listened."

There's no apology in his voice, no softness, no care, only this cold, hard fact he just uttered. I should've listened. But words are one thing, and how his loving arms felt around me was so real and so right. So very right, it feels like someone died now that he's shown me this side of him. This thing that makes him almost exactly like all the other assholes in my life up until now.

Tonight he didn't rape me, but he's probably just one of those who gear up to it slowly, after first reeling me in with soft kisses and loving ways. And that just makes him the worst dog of them all. Because he showed me everything is possible, but now he's gonna just take it away before he even gives me more than a taste.

I have nothing to say to him. And I don't get a chance to try either, because the door is already closing behind him. Maybe he's never coming back. Maybe I won't be here when he does.

But, damn it, I start missing him two seconds after he's gone, and all my well laid plans of leaving him before he got violent, before it got painful and hurtful, all pretty much left with him. Because I'm an idiot who keeps making the same mistake over and over again, keeps falling for the wrong guy over and over again, and expects to force love where there's none to give.

But not this time.

This time I'm gonna get out while most of the memories are still good. Even this one will turn good in time, because he stopped when I asked him to. But next time he might not stop, and then the good memories we made will be ruined forever. I can live with a lot, but I know I couldn't live with that. So I'm leaving instead.

## 15

Ice

OF ALL THE things she could've called me, she went with dog. She's been so good at saying the perfect thing all the time, in any situation, and then she went with dog. It took me right back to my cell, which was just four concrete walls, a wooden bench to sleep on, and no light apart from the thin sliver of it under the metal door that was kept bolted shut except when Lizard brought me the food I wouldn't eat.

"Start eating and start fighting for me," he'd keep telling me in that sickly sweet voice of his, which I suppose worked better on the women he was trying to break elsewhere, in other cells like the one he kept me in. It didn't work on me though.

"Things will get better for you once you start fighting for me," he'd also tell me. "It's your only way out. You lived this long, you don't wanna die now."

Then they forced the food down my throat. It went on forever. All I wanted was to rip his throat out. But he knew that, so he kept my hands chained up.

And he just kept coming, kept making me promises in that sickly sweet voice, kept making me eat, kept making me look at his ugly face until my need to kill him trumped even my wish to not exist anymore. So I started eating on my own. Off the floor like a dog, because I had no use of my hands. And I fought. And won every fight. Like a good dog.

After that, they did unchain me and they did give me a bigger cell with a better bed and a table to eat off. But it was still just four concrete walls and no windows. It soon grew so full of my hate for them all there was no room for anything else in it. Not even for me.

Sometimes the fog of hate lifted long enough to show me that they had broken me, that I was just Lizard's dog and that he'd kill me once I was no longer useful to him. So I kept winning the fights, because my revenge waited at the end of them, and I had to live to get it.

But I was just a beaten, broken dog long before the Devils freed me and gave me my revenge.

And she reminded me spectacularly well of that tonight, just as spectacularly well as she showed me all those other things I forgot I ever wanted while the hate was all there was.

So I showed her what she called up this time. Almost. It took a lot, yet I managed to stop the monster from coming out.

But the problem started before she called me a dog tonight. I didn't even see her very clearly anymore by the time we got to the motel room. She's the best thing that could've still happened to me, yet she's also the one thing who could destroy everything I do still have. Destroy Roxie's family and mine all over again.

At first, I tried hard to stay human while they kept me locked up, only letting me out to fight in a cage, but that was a pipe dream from the start. Before long, it was easier to let go of all dreams except the one of revenge, easier to become the animal they treated me like. It was kill or be killed in the cage, and I survived, got strong and mean, so I could one day make my one dream come true. Somewhere along the way I forgot what it felt like to be human. I forgot I wasn't just a dog in human form.

She made me remember though. She showed me the man I used to be, the man I wanted to become before I couldn't anymore. And that man I never got to be would never hurt a woman, and certainly not her, the sweetest, purest, and most beautiful woman I've ever met.

But he's still just a memory, just an echo from the past, which right now tastes about as bitter as this beer I'm trying to drink.

She deserves better than me. And she deserves to be treated better by me. I'm glad I managed to remember that before I fucked her in the ass tonight. For these last few days, she's given me something I thought I'd never have again. I can't keep it, but I can't just fling that gift back at her face either. What I have to do is thank her for it.

I toss some money on the counter to pay for my half-finished beer and walk out of the bar before I change my mind again. She deserves an apology and a thank you, but it'd be better if she were gone when I got back to the room. For her, for my sister, for everyone. Maybe I should be the one to just leave tonight. But I can't do that, I made her a promise to take her to the ocean and I'm the kinda guy who always keeps his promises.

Though if I give her some more time to think about it, then maybe she'll realize it'd be better for her if she didn't hold me to it.

With that in mind, I pull into a gas station that's not far from our motel. Or did I stop, because I want to get her some flowers or candy, or something else that'll tell her how sorry I am, because I'll probably do a shit job of telling her? But the wilted, dead from the heat flowers they sell here won't do a much better job of that either, and all the candy just looks cheap.

I get stuck in front of the jewelry display, trying to pick something out and wondering if I should at all. I've never gotten jewelry for a woman before and giving her one of these earrings or necklaces will probably give her the wrong idea, but I want to bring her something nicer than wilted flowers or cheap candy.

Finally, I just snatch up one of the gold necklaces with a heart dangling off it and bring it to the register, because that's enough thinking. If they had one with a butterfly pendant, I'd get her that, but they don't. This looks exactly like the heart she has tattooed on her hand, but a whole one, so she'll probably be happy with it. I hope I didn't hurt her too bad before, but I probably did. She was crying for fuck's sake. But women cry, it's what they do.

Not Barbie though, she doesn't cry just for the hell of it. And I know that for a fact, so I also know I must've hurt her real bad to make her cry and beg me to stop.

She's sitting in the window, staring at me as I approach the room and that hurt is all I see. But I fucking warned her. More than once. The light is on and she's dressed for the road—jeans, boots, jacket and the scarf that gypsy gave her. Guess it wasn't enough to protect her from me like that crazy old fraud hoped.

"I'm sorry, Barbie," I tell her once I stop in front of her.

The plastic bag with her clothes and stuff is all packed up and sitting on the floor next to her. She was getting ready to leave, and that makes me angry and sad at the same time. It wouldn't be a relief if I found her gone, and I know that very clearly right now.

Yet she didn't leave and she's just staring at me now. I have no idea what's going on behind those brilliant blue eyes of hers. Those sparkling, pretty eyes that still make me wish I could be the guy for her as they've done since I first noticed her.

## BARBIE

I DIDN'T EXPECT him to come back. And I certainly didn't expect him to apologize. I expected him to tell me it was all my fault and go to sleep if and when he came back. The thought that I'd believe he was sincere if he did apologize, never even crossed my mind. And I've been lied to a lot, so I know what sincere looks like.

He's looking into my eyes, waiting for me to say something, but I'll be damned if I know what. Sure, there's literally thousands of things I could say flying through my brain, there always is at any given moment, because I'm a chatterbox, but I don't know which one's the right one to say in this situation.

"Were you leaving?" he asks.

I take my legs off the windowsill, but I don't stand up, and I don't get any closer to him.

"I was gonna, yeah," I say.

I had decided to go, but the moments just kept ticking by, while I stayed put. After an hour, I was sure he wasn't coming back, and I didn't want to witness that, I wanted to be gone before I *knew* that he could just leave me behind. That would spoil the good memories too.

"You should've," he says.

"Is that what you wanted?" I snap. "Is that why you...why you..." I wanna say *almost raped me*, but that's such a big and heavy accusation, and I don't want it hanging between us along with all the other things already there that are preventing us from accepting what I know we have—the kind of love that only comes once in a lifetime, if at all.

He sits next to me on the windowsill, but not close enough for our legs to touch. "You shouldn't have called me a dog. I spent six years of my life living like the worst kept dog, and feeling less than one most of the time. At least they keep the fighter dogs with other dogs. Me, I was alone in a window- less room all the time. The only time I was near other people was when I had to beat someone up, or when a Spawn decided it'd be fun to taunt me. I held out as long as I could, but there's nothing human or noble in any of that. It's just hell on earth. I'd let them kill me, but I needed to get my revenge first. "

He pauses, breathing heavily and looking deeply into my eyes, but I'm not sure he's seeing me, I think he's just seeing all those horrible things he just told me about.

"I don't want to hurt you, Barbie," he adds, proving me wrong that he doesn't see me. He sees me very clearly, sees only me right now, and exactly the way I always wanted to be seen. "But it's gonna happen. It almost happened tonight. Because they broke me."

He's so sure of that, but I know he's wrong. I lay my palm on his cheek, because whatever else is going on, I need to be touching him. I'll always need that, and I didn't know it this clearly until this very moment.

"They didn't break you. I've seen broken and you're not it," I say, thinking of all those women who had it way worse than me, thinking of my mother who was completely broken from the drugs and all those men she let use her body to feed her habit until there was nothing left. "Broken people don't love, they don't help strangers out of kindness, they don't care about anything or anyone, they're just numb. You're not like that. You just lost yourself, and forgot the man you were. But you're still that man deep down. "

He shakes his head and moves his face away from my hand like he can't stand my touch, like he doesn't want me touching him. And that hurts too much.

"I'm sorry I said what I said. It's something I'd say to men in the past, bad men who hurt me and pissed me off, and I shouldn't have said it to you," I tell him. "You're a good man. I'm sorry I hurt you."

He snorts a laugh. "You're apologizing to me? Come on, Barbie, have more self-respect than that. I snapped because I'm not right in the head, and you can expect more of that sort of thing if you stick around. You're wrong. I'm not a good man. I'm not even sure I'm a man anymore."

I wish he'd kiss me, because then everything would be alright again. I wish he'd at least take my hand. But he's not moving.

"You're the best man I've ever met," I whisper, and I was gonna go on, but he grimaces so I don't.

"You know what I was thinking when I first noticed you in that bar?" he asks but not like he's expecting an answer, so I don't speak. "I was thinking I should've died that night when all my brothers and my father died. I was also thinking that I can die now that I've avenged them all. Then you crashed into my life, and things got wild for awhile, but I'm still right where I was. Not fit for this world. And if tonight didn't convince you—"

I lay my fingers over his lips to silence him.

"You know what, Ice, you chose your fate and you did what you had to do to survive. You went into captivity to save your sister, and then you came out and punished everyone who wronged you. But now you're free, so be free. I get it, because I chose my life too, every step of the way I chose it, right up until the moment my last boyfriend tried to sell me off to another guy and I chose to run away with you instead. And I keep choosing it, even though I'm now stuck with nothing and fighting for the love of a man who keeps pushing me away. But, yeah, we both chose this, so lets be grown up and own it."

I didn't pause at all, so he wouldn't get the chance to interrupt me before I had my say. I'm breathing hard now as I try to see if my words had any effect. He's looking at me sharply like he's gonna say something mean, but then his eyes turn thoughtful. And the longer they stay locked on mine, the softer they grow.

"You have a point, I'll give you that, but that's just a bunch of words. The reality of it is what happened before, it's what could still happen."

I suppose he means to tell me again that the sum total of all that reality is me being better off staying away from him. But he's wrong.

"I love you, Ice, with all my heart," I tell him. I've spent these last few days getting up the courage to tell him that. It was easier to say it than I thought it would be. Much easier. I'm looking so deep into his eyes I can see all the way to the distant snow-capped horizon in them.

But he's not saying anything back. I'm not even sure he can see me.

"I know," he finally says. "But you're wrong."

"How can I be wrong about how I feel?" I say,

since I expected this to go a lot differently than it has. I expected him to kiss me and tell me he loves me with all his heart too, because I know he does.

He reaches into his pocket and hands me something gold and shiny.

"I got this for you to show you I was sorry," he says, totally evading my question.

It's a heart, one of those you can break in two, so each of the lovers can keep their half, and exactly like the one I have tattooed on my hand. He won't say he loves me, but he goes and buys me this? Reality isn't what he's saying it is, because he can't see it, he's hiding from it. This necklace is our reality.

I take it and snap it in half, giving him his. "Here, half of it is yours. Forever."

He stares at it with a very puzzled look in his eyes, but doesn't take it. So I just place it into his hand and close his fingers around it.

"You already have my heart, you'll always have it," I say. "You can tell me I'm wrong all you want, but it's how I feel."

Then I stand up and take off my jacket and my scarf.

"Now come to bed with me, so you can show me what you won't say to me. I'm a simple girl, I don't need words. Actions are enough."

He pulls me back as I take the first step, wraps his arms around me and kisses me so deeply and so lovingly the ground feels like water beneath my feet. We don't need the beach, because we already found our ocean. The words will come too.

I've won my argument, even if he can't say it yet. And I didn't lie before. I don't need words. I need his kisses, and his arms holding me tight, and him to hold. We'll just figure out the rest one step at a time.

## 16

ICE

SHE SEEMS to have forgiven me, both for what I did, and for being dismissive when she told me she loved me. At least I think so, because her kisses still taste just as sweet. But I haven't forgiven myself.

We didn't fuck after that long, draining conversation last night, nor this morning, and I should stop kissing her too, because I'm just giving her false hope at this point. I know this must end. There's no other way. And I knew that before I even stepped in to prevent those old-timers from hitting her.

But it's not easy knowing it with her arms wrapped around my waist, her head resting against my back and her hands stroking my stomach under my shirt. All of that's just making me wish another outcome was possible. Looking into her beautiful turquoise eyes does the same thing. As does kissing her.

I couldn't not bring her to Sanctuary either. Cross told me to come there, and he may not be my president, but ignoring a direct request like that from him is also not how it works. That man has done too much for me to disrespect his wishes. He gave me my life back, such as it is, and he gave me my revenge on the Spawns. Maybe he can even help me figure out how to keep Barbie safe from that old man of hers, and the one he wants to give her to. But I'm not letting him risk anything or anyone to achieve it.

I already made that decision when I saved her.

All day, a nagging voice in the back of my head's been telling me I can keep her safe. That I need no one to help me do that. Nagging at me to keep her close because she's the best I ever had. But I rode fast and it's faded to a whisper now. That was the old Ice talking, the guy who did die in the rain on that night seven years ago whatever Barbie believes. This guy that survived won't ever lose anything again.

"Is that it?" she asks, or gasps more like. We're

almost at the metal gate in the wall that surrounds Sanctuary.

"Yeah," I tell her.

"Walls like that will keep anyone out," she adds, and I can hear how much she wants that, what being protected like that means to her, and she deserves it too. Again, I'm not the guy for that.

We haven't discussed anything about the future apart from me telling her we'll be making a stop here. She hasn't asked any questions, and she hasn't been talking much either. Maybe she hasn't really forgiven me. It'd be for the best that way.

Four is on the gate, as is the norm, since watching the gate is pretty much the sum total of his duties for the MC now that he's too old for anything else. He opens the gate for us and lets us enter without saying anything.

We left the motel early in the morning and the sun's already set now. The garden around the Devil's Nightmare MC HQ building—a mansion by no stretch of the word—is washed in shadows and looks so peaceful. The huge garden surrounding it is like that too. I always see that kinda peaceful shit everywhere. It's because I've been looking for peace so hard.

"Is this like some castle or something?" Barbie exclaims as she gets off the bike. She nearly trips on her own feet, because she's checking out the building so intently.

The hot pants she's wearing barely cover her ass, and the top she has on under her jacket doesn't leave much to the imagination either. She'll make quite a splash here in that outfit, as the two guys gawking at her from the garage off to the side of the main building are already proving.

Rumor has it that this place used to be full of club whores back in the day before Cross' daughter came to live with him. That must've been something, the way the guys tell it. But now the women have all been confined to the clubhouse in town, which is still a fun place, if you're looking for that kinda thing. I had plans to leave Barbie there to find someone else, but with Brick looking for her here, I'd better not.

Though maybe I should've left her there just for the duration of this visit. Roxie came out to greet us with a huge smile, which quickly turned into this stern, sour expression on her face now, as she watches Barbie take in everything there is to see. She was always too critical of the women I chose to be with. A born old lady, that's what she always was, and it used to piss me off then just like it's doing now.

I put my arm around Barbie's shoulders, the

sudden need to let everyone know she's with me overwhelming, even though it's pointless.

"Come, meet my sister," I tell her.

She's all smiles for Roxie, whose brooding face does soften a little, because it's impossible not to react that way to Barbie's smiles. They're too bright.

"I heard a lot about you," Barbie says, squeezing her hand firmly in both of hers.

Roxie nods and even cracks a tiny smile, then turns to me. "I'm glad you're home, Ice."

"I wouldn't call it home, Rox," I tell her. "Where's Cross?"

I wanna get this over with fast. Just thinking about what I'm gonna do after this meeting has been making me sick all day, but there's no other way. This may not be my home, but it's Roxie's home, it's the home of her unborn child, my nephew's home, and I won't do anything to fuck that up.

"I think he's in his office," she says, and I guide Barbie towards her then remove my arm from her shoulders.

"Get her something to eat," I tell Roxie.

They're both looking at me sharply, but I'm avoiding both their gazes, especially Barbie's. There's almost no light out here anymore, and nothing has color, but her eyes are electric blue anyway. Letting her go seems impossible, but so was taking her when I had no right to.

I don't say anything more, just go in search of Cross to get this over with.

He's alone in his office, sitting at his desk, but he was expecting me. He probably saw us arrive on the cameras.

"Welcome back, Ice," he says and gets up to fix himself a drink. I nod when he motions if I'd like one, though it would take that whole bottle to take the edge off tonight, or more like a couple of bottles.

"I ain't staying," I tell him and don't move from beside the door as though to prove what I just said.

"You're both welcome to stay, if you want. As long as you follow the rules," he says as he hands me the glass of Scotch. I drink it in one go, don't even feel the burn.

"We're a danger to you here," I say. "It's best I disappear. I only came because you told me to, but I shouldn't have. I don't want to bring any problems down on you. I've done enough of that already."

He's giving me one of those hard black stares he's famous for.

"I get it, Ice," he says finally. "You lost a lot. But if you want to keep this woman, we'll help you keep her. I've spoken to the guys and they agree. And the offer to join us as a full brother is still open. We all agree on that too."

I shake my head, clutching my empty glass so hard I'm surprised it hasn't shattered yet. "With all due respect, Cross, you don't get it and I'm glad you don't. You've all put yourself in enough danger too many times for me, and I'll be damned if I ask it of you again. Not for something I'm not even fit to keep."

I said too much, but fuck it, this feels like the night to do that.

"I'll face the men who want her back and I'll do it alone. She'll be out of their reach by then," I add. "There'll be no need for you or anyone else to get involved. And afterwards, if I live, I'll disappear too."

"No offense to your father, but we're not easily messed with," he says. "Have no fear that if we take on a job, we see it through successfully. And I'm sure this one will be a breeze."

I have plenty of fear, and regret, and anger that things are as they are. But I won't contradict him, because I know he's right. They'll win this fight, if I ask them to take it on, but at what cost? And Barbie deserves better than me.

"This is my fight, Cross," I tell him. "I appreciate all you've done for me, and all you're still willing to do, but you're not my president and this is my problem to solve."

A fucking mountain of a problem is what this is. More than one man can handle. But it has to be done, and I'm hardly a man anymore.

"Just join us, Ice," Cross says as though I didn't bluntly refuse him two minutes ago.

My answer is still the same. "No."

"The lone wolf doesn't survive the winter," he says, and it's a fitting reference but fucking painful too.

"I died a long time ago, Cross. I died with all the other wolves that night."

He shakes his head. "This is too deep for me, man. But I see you're still alive, and that's something I do understand."

I shrug, because as far as I'm concerned we've said all that needs to be said tonight.

"According to Hawk, the Bloods and the Kings are close by, poking around for news of the woman they're looking for. They haven't entered Pleasantville yet, and they've made no more phone calls, but they brought numbers, so they mean business," Cross says.

"I'll take care of it, and we'll be leaving now," I say and deposit the empty glass I've been rolling around in my hands on the cupboard by the door.

It seems time's running out. I have to get Barbie away from here, hide her somewhere where she'll be protected and as far from me and my rotten self as possible. I'm ready to die so the Bloods and the Kings never find her again, but that's all I can offer her.

BARBIE

"So, how did you and Ice meet?" Roxie asks just as I'm about to bite into the sandwich she made for me.

This question has been on the tip of her tongue, while she insisted she didn't need any help as she prepared my food. She also kept glancing at my outfit, her eyes screaming disapproval, so it's real surprising she managed not to cut herself. But her eyes cut me up plenty. I was hands-shaking nervous about meeting her all the way here. I hoped she'd like me, and I still hope she'll grow to like me, but it's not looking promising.

I chew fast. "We met at Boar's Pit Stop, it's this bar in—"

"I know it," she says curtly, but I don't think that tone's just aimed at me. Of course she knows it, she grew up in that town, just like Ice, and she lost her entire family there too. I should cut her some slack.

I do look like some club slut in this outfit, while she's the old lady of the president of one of the most powerful clubs in the country. And I'm with her brother. Of course she's looking down on me. It's what all old ladies do, it comes with the territory. But I'll win her over.

"Anyway, he helped me out of a tight spot with my ex," I tell her. "And we've just been riding across the country ever since. It was the best time I ever had. You're brother's a great guy."

She nods, her eyes turning kinda sad. "He is."

I take another bite of my sandwich, not sure if I should tell her anything more. Ice has been so distant all day. He wouldn't make love to me, but he held me and kissed me all night. I know he's truly sorry about snapping, and I won't lie that it didn't feel rotten. But I've had so much worse, and I've never had better than the good times we shared on the road. That part's no lie.

"I love him. And I think he loves me too," I tell her, not even sure why, but, somehow, I'm sure she needs to know it.

She finally smiles for the first time, and even though it's a sad little smile, it still brightens up her face considerably.

"I hoped he'd find someone," she says. "He's been so cold and untouchable...not the man I remember at all."

"Sometimes he is that man," I tell her because I'm sure I'm right. "When he forgets about what he went through, he's the best man I know."

And I've known a lot of men. But I don't tell her that, although going by that discerning look in her eyes, she's already thinking it anyway.

"All I want is for him to be happy," she says.

"Me too."

Then I start eating and apart from me telling her the sandwich is tasty, we don't talk anymore. I hope Ice will come find me soon. I'd like to help him forget tonight, because I've had no luck all day.

"Are you ready?" he asks from the doorway behind my back. I turn to him and nod with a big smile on my face.

He doesn't smile back. "Let's go then."

"To the beach?" I ask as I join him by the door.

The longer I look at his face, the less I want to keep smiling. I thought I've seen all the winter he carries inside him, but this look on his face takes it to a whole new level of freezing.

"We'll see," he says.

"I'll talk to you later, Roxie," he says to his sister, as he lets me out of the room.

I don't hear her reply, and I can't really see anything around me. I only see his back as he overtakes me on the way to the front door. I don't know what to think, let alone what to say, but the sight of his back is significant, I'm sure of that. Because everything feels like it's crumbling again and not just a little bit. This is the destructive and loud kind of crumbling that leaves nothing whole.

# 17

BARBIE

IT'S full dark by the time we stop at a bar that's way off the beaten track, up on a hill, next to a country road and surrounded by a thick forest. It's called the Saloon, music is blaring inside it, people are shouting, and the parking lot's full of bikes. I've spent my entire adult life in places like this. But tonight feels like that first night I entered one, when I was seventeen and this life of mine began.

I have nothing against bars like this, it's wild and free and uninhibited in there, all I ever wanted out of life. But I don't want to go in tonight. I'm ready to leave it all behind with Ice. Yet, I precede him inside anyway.

I don't stick out in here, I'm right where I belong. The place is full of bikers, old, young and in between, and the girls are all dressed in some variant of what I'm wearing. A couple of them are kissing and undressing each other by a pole in the center of the room, and I'm pretty sure the guys forming a tight circle around them, as they watch will all pounce on them once the last garment falls, and then this will turn into an orgy. Like I said, I've been here before, and I've seen it all. But I can't figure out why I'm here again. This is the first biker bar we stopped at on our way out West.

"Why did we come here?" I ask once we're sitting at a small table near the door. The tabletop is littered with empty beer bottles and sticky with spilt booze. My chair is sticky too.

The men are turning in our direction, and though most of them are checking me out, they're all paying Ice more attention.

He ignores them all, even the ones calling out his name and raising their drinks to him. He's ignoring my question too.

"Talk to me, Ice," I say. It's the first time I've demanded this of him, even though his silences usually drag on and on. He's never given me such an icy stare, as the one he's giving me now that his eyes are finally meeting mine.

"We had a good run, Barbie. But it's over now," he says and my heart stops beating. Just goes dead still in my chest, filling with unpumped blood until it explodes.

A waitress is standing by my side watching me questioningly, but I don't know how to speak anymore.

"Bring us a couple of beers," Ice tells her, calm as you like, as though he didn't just shatter my heart into a million sharp little pieces.

"What...What do you mean?" Him saying that makes no sense, none whatsoever.

"I mean what I said," he says and at least he's not repeating those dream-shattering words again, so there's that.

"How, Ice? You love me, I know you do. How can you just walk away from me?" I don't even feel pathetic saying this, because I know it's true.

Plenty of guys fell in love with me over the years, and plenty fell out of love with me too. But him, no, I never saw him do that. I only saw him fall *in* love with me.

He snatches his bottle of beer right off the tray as the waitress brings it, and drinks more than half of it before she even sets mine down on the table.

"I don't wanna discuss it, Barbie. You'll find someone else," he says. "You're not safe with me, and no one's safe if we stay together. If that boyfriend of yours is willing to come all the way out to Cali to get you back then there's probably something still there. Maybe you can even go back with him. Or you can find someone else here. A beauty like you will have no problem with that. He won't wander into this place, since only the locals know it, so you have time to think about what you want to do next."

"You've given this a lot of thought," I say and drink some of my beer because my throat is very dry. So dry, it hurts to talk. But everything about this hurts and the beer won't help. "When were you gonna tell me Brick is out here looking for me?"

The winter in his eyes falters just a little. "I'm telling you now. I only just learned tonight that he's close. You should stay hidden. Find someone who'll protect you."

"You'll protect me," I say quietly. I was so sure that was a done deal already, that I still can't make sense of any of this.

"No, I can't."

He puts the plastic bag with my clothes on the table. I didn't even notice him bring it in.

"How does this work in your mind, Ice? Please explain it to me," I snap, eyeing the bag with my stuff like it's a rattlesnake readying to bite me. "How can you just leave me? I took you for a braver man than that."

Now I'm just getting nasty, because in my heart, I already know there's no more talking about this. He's made up his mind.

"You wanna know how it works?" he asks, his voice finally getting some color. "Alright, I'll tell you. All I've been seeing all day today are my dead brothers in the burning building where they died. Along with the picture of a brutally murdered woman Lizard told me was my sister. I won't risk that happening again. Once was enough. You're a great girl. But you're also a great big danger of history repeating itself. "

He said those last few sentences in that wintery calm way of his, but the emotion behind them shook me to the core anyway. How do I argue with that? How do I ask him to risk it all for me?

"I love you and you love me." I say, reaching for his hand, but he snatches it away before I can take hold of it.

"And love is the greatest force in this world, it can overcome anything," I finish my thought anyway, quietly, because I might as well be saying it to a mountain of snow.

He doesn't reply, doesn't even look at me, as he

pulls out his wallet, but his hand is shaking a little as he opens it. Or maybe it just looks that way because my eyes are filling with tears.

He pulls out a fistful of money and holds it out to me. "Take this to get started."

I shake my head hard and reach into the plastic bag, looking for the red dress I wore when we met. "No, keep your money. In fact, take this back too."

I toss the three hundred dollars I took from him on that day he gave me his wallet to go shopping. If I could go back to that day right now I would, in a second. But I wouldn't change a damn thing that happened afterwards. I'd just fall in love with him all over again.

"I don't want your money, I just want you," I say, while he's looking at the cash on the table like this is the first time he's seeing money.

"You don't want me, Barbie. You just fell for some idea of me, because I acted like a knight on a white horse come to rescue you," he says, some fire creeping back into his voice. "But you've seen what I'm really like, and that ain't changing. You will find someone better. You're a sweet, kind and giving girl, and you deserve better than me. If you stay with me, I'll just destroy you, and other people will get hurt too. I can't have either of those things on my conscience."

I take his hand before he can grab the bottle to finish his drink. "You're wrong. Well, maybe not entirely. What you did for me on the night we met is more than any guy's ever done for me, but that's not what made me fall in love with you. I fell in love with the man you showed me you are on our ride. The caring and considerate man you truly are. You had a hard life, I get that, believe me I understand it, but the bad's over now, it's in the past and you have your whole life in front of you. Brick won't move against the Devils. The mere sight of them will make him turn around and ride back to Illinois. Trust me, he's not a brave man."

His eyes aren't as hard anymore, as he takes my hand in both of his and squeezes like I've finally won him over.

"I love you, Ice, and I want to spend the rest of my life with you," I say and this time, regardless of all he said before, I'm expecting him to say it back. Everything in his face, his eyes most of all, are telling me he's about to.

So the shock as he releases my hand, gets up and just walks out paralyzes me completely. I don't even fully comprehend it's happening until the door is closing behind him. I can't let him go.

I grab my stuff and the money and run outside, reach him as he's already mounting his bike.

LENA BOURNE

"This is such bullshit, Ice!" I say. "Don't just walk away, please."

I'm all out of arguments, this is all I have left.

He gets off his bike, grabs me roughly by the waist and pulls me into the best kiss I've ever had. Raw and wild and filled to the brim with all the sweetness, all the freedom, and all the joy this world has to offer. I swear I can even hear birds singing, and butterflies flapping their wings, even though it's the dead of night and the only butterflies awake are those his kiss woke in my stomach. He's holding me tight too, so tight I'm having trouble inhaling, but I don't need to breathe, I just need him.

No one will ever convince me this isn't love. You don't hold someone like this, you don't kiss them like this, if you don't love them. It's not possible.

But then he releases me and I stagger because I was leaning on him and he just took away my support. He gets back on his bike.

"Goodbye, Barbie," he says and drives off, gunning it before I can find my voice.

"No! You can't go!" I yell after him, but it's too late, I can't even see his taillights through the trees anymore.

The music in the bar behind me is still blaring, people are still shouting and everything about this place feels like a second home to me. But he felt more like home than any place I've ever lived in. I've been dumped like this before, had to start all over just like this many times before. I could turn around, go back into the bar and find a man to ride off with later tonight, once the party's over. I'm good at that, I've done it time and time again.

But the only man I ever want to ride anywhere with isn't in there. He drove off into the night without me and my heart is aching so bad I just want to cry from now until forever.

He promised to take me to the ocean and he didn't. His kisses and his embraces promised me he'd never let me go, but he did.

One glance over my shoulder at the bar is all it takes for me to know I won't go back in tonight. My old life is in there, and it holds nothing for me anymore.

I'll go see the ocean on my own, it can't be far now, and maybe the walk will help. I don't imagine it will, but I have to keep moving forward, because there's no going back for me. The way forward doesn't look very hopeful right now either. Ice took the last bits of my heart into the night with him.

Only it wasn't just bits anymore, it was my whole heart, the one I thought I lost forever long ago. He gave that back to me, and now he took it with him. I should hate him for it, but it just hurts and I just love him. This doesn't feel real.

---

## ICE

I DON'T REMEMBER the ride back to Sanctuary at all. The first thing that registers, since I last looked into Barbie's sad eyes, which were bright blue despite the darkness, are Roxie's stern ones.

"Where's Barbie?" she asks as I pass her on the way up to my room.

"She's gone," I mutter and keep walking. Saying it feels like I'm chewing rocks. But what the fuck else could I do? Go around riding with her on the back of my bike until everyone I know got killed all over again trying to protect us?

"I wish you'd talk to me, Brandon," she calls after me. She only ever uses my real name when she'd absolutely had it with me. But I couldn't care less if that's the case right now. I don't care about anything right now. I hardly even heard her speak.

Barbie's pleading voice as she begged me to stay is the only thing I hear clearly. A strong woman like her begging…I never wanted to hear that. And now I'll never unhear it.

"There's nothing to say, Roxie," I mutter and enter my room.

She must've been waiting up for me to get back, but we'll have to talk some other time. Or never. Because I'm not lying, there is nothing to say.

I did what I had to do. I made the only decision I can live with. The only one that'll let me go on with this life, which I wouldn't even call that.

The only life I want to live is the one with Barbie.

That nagging voice in the back of my head has been telling me this all through my ride back here alone. But I've ignored it, and it's starting to fade. I'm almost back in that state of black nothingness where I spent most of my captivity. Where nothing means anything.

I won't watch anyone else I love die. I can't. Leaving Barbie is hard, but it's easier.

Barbie

I WALKED ALL NIGHT. The road kept going up and each hill I crested showed me another I needed to climb, while hiding the ocean from me. So I kept climbing the hills, kept hoping the next one will show me the ocean.

The whole thing was kinda like my life so far. I keep climbing hill after hill, only to be disappointed when I get to the top, only to see another one I still have to climb, only to end up right at the beginning once I do. Except the hills in my life are actually men.

On this last hill I just climbed, I found the sea. It's

just a splash of blue on the horizon, rippling in this half-light of dawn, and way too far to walk to. And that's very much like meeting Ice, the man I know is the love of my life. But he's gone now, impossible for me to reach. Hell, I can't even watch him from a distance, the way I can watch the ocean right now.

I used to get sad when I was younger, while I was growing up with a junkie for a mom, a stepdad who started fucking me before I even knew what sex was, and a grandma who couldn't do anything about any of it. But then, I decided that being sad gets you nowhere. It doesn't get you out of bed in the morning, and it makes it hard to keep putting one foot in front of the other even if you do.

I wish I'd told Ice that. I wish I could've made him believe it. I didn't though and now he's gone, and I wish I could hate him. Hell, I wish I could at least be angry with him. But I'm just sad.

It's OK though, I'll just sleep. My legs and my feet are killing me from all that walking. When I wake up, the sun will be up and I'll see the ocean more clearly. I made it here, with little help from a man. After my baby died I slept for weeks, like a butterfly sleeps in its cocoon before it becomes the most beautiful and delicate thing in the world. I'll sleep, and then I'll get up and go on. Just like I've always done.

## ICE

FALLING ASLEEP WAS HARD, but waking up is harder. I reached for her before I even opened my eyes, because I'm so used to having her by my side, and because the first thought in my brain when I regained awareness in the mornings was the need to touch her.

That need is burning through me worse than a forest fire as I realize she's gone.

My reasons for leaving her last night are still solid, still the insurmountable mountains they were from the start, still as immovable.

But my need to have her with me right now is a raging fire.

Waking up in that cell they kept me locked up in was easier than this. Even after all hope of ever getting free was swallowed up by the black nothingness, and each morning was just a fresh reminder of the hopelessness of it all. I wish the black nothingness would come back now. But the fire's too bright. And too hot.

I didn't undress before getting into bed last night, so I just get up and leave the room. I have to get moving, go do something, anything, but be alone with my thoughts.

I was alone with my thoughts for so fucking long, it became the only thing I knew. But then she came with all her talking, and all her perfect things to say. I can't be alone with these new thoughts, can't be alone with memories of her, I'll lose what's left of my mind if I try.

"Where's the woman?" Cross asks. Him and Roxie are standing at the foot of the stairs. They just had breakfast, probably, and now she's going to rest, because I'm pretty sure she's about to have the baby any day now. At least I hope she needs to go lie down. Because I don't want to talk.

"I let her go," I say, but that's a lie. I'll never let her go. But I had to set her free.

"I left her at the Saloon," I elaborate as I descend the stairs, since they're both looking at me for more of an explanation. "I pissed her off pretty bad, so it's more than likely she'll find that old boyfriend of hers and get back with him on her own. Either way, she's not your problem anymore."

It's making me sick saying that, and makes me see red imagining it. That was my plan and I carried it out and now it's done. She's not coming back. But I hope to hell she never gets back with that abusive motherfucker I took her from.

"I'll get in touch with him and meet him some-where, so we can talk this out just to make sure everything is squared away now," I add as I join them in the hall.

They're both looking at me like they're seeing me for the first time, especially Roxie, and I hate it when she looks at me like that. She's been doing it a lot though, most of the fucking time actually, since I've been back.

"I can't let you do that on your own, Ice," Cross says. "They'll kill you for what you did."

"You don't command me, Cross," I say harshly. "This is my choice and my decision."

"Ice, you can't," Roxie says, her voice all shaky like she's about to start crying. She used to do a lot of that, always was volatile with tears as far back as I can remember, but it has no effect on me anymore. The fire's burned out. Now there's just hot, angry ash left. Once that cools off, there'll be nothing left.

"I was so happy when you came back with a woman," Roxie says. "And she seemed so good for you."

"Come on, Rox, let's not lie to each other now. You thought she was trash from the second you saw her," I snap, ignoring Cross' black look. She was my sister before she was his old lady, so I'll have none of his "I'm her old man" protectiveness over her now.

"Fine, Brandon, yeah, I judged her based on how she was dressed," Roxie says angrily, because she's never needed anyone to fight her battles. "But then I spoke to her, and I saw that what you two had was real. I believed her when she spoke about loving you and you loving her. So just stop, Ice, just stop rushing off into destruction, when so many people want you to live. Don't fight the good just because you can't stop seeing the bad. It's done, it's in the past, let it go. Please."

"It's not in the past, Roxie, it's all there is," I say. "I'm glad you could let go of the past, but there's no going back for me."

"So go forward," she interjects.

"Listen to your sister, Ice," Cross says, and if he's mocking Roxie's woman logic, I can't hear it in his voice. "We're all here for you."

I could say more, could explain all the ways in which what they're asking me to do is impossible. I have no heart left. What remained of it, I left with Barbie at that bar. It wasn't much, but it was something, and it was all hers, because she's the one who found it after I was sure there wasn't anything to find.

I could explain all that to them, but what's the point?

Roxie suddenly grabs her stomach and grunts in pain.

"What's wrong?" Cross asks in alarm and despite the frost in my chest, my heart's beating very fast in fear too. Roxie's face is all contorted like she's in a lot of pain.

"It's happening, I think," she says through gritted teeth. "Our son is coming, get Doc."

Cross rushes off to do that, and she grabs hold of my arm.

"Stop fighting, Ice, you don't need to fight anymore," she says in a quiet voice, then grimaces again and exhales sharply.

"I need you, your nephew needs you, that girl needs you, and you need you," she continues once she recovers again. "What's done is done, and not a day goes by that I don't miss Dad and everyone. Not a day went by that I didn't miss you, but now you're back. So please, be back. Stay. Don't make me miss you again."

Her face contorts again and she's gripping my arm so hard her fingers are cutting off the circulation to my hand. Beads of sweat are erupting on her forehead, so I reach into my pocket to get the bandana the Devils gave me to hide my face during the jobs we did together, and that I never used. But as I do, my finger catches on the sharp edge of the broken half heart pendant Barbie made me take. Even my sister's very obvious extreme pain fades as the memory of that night erupts in my mind. Barbie gave me her heart that night. Despite seeing who I really am, despite me pushing her away. And she didn't take it back last night.

I'm an idiot for chasing her away. She's the best thing I've ever gotten in my life, both before Lizard and certainly after. Don't know why I needed my sister yelling at me to finally see this, but then again, I've always been slow on the uptake.

I can't say anything, because things are finally falling into their right place in my brain. Or maybe they've been in the right place for awhile now, and just the blackness is lifting from my mind, because I haven't seen things this clearly in a long time. I need to get Barbie back.

Cross and Doc are rushing towards us and I get her to release my arm.

"You're in good hands now, Roxie," I say as I hand her over to Cross.

"How are you feeling?" Doc asks her.

She gives him a crooked smile, her teeth firmly gritted together. "It hurts like I'm having my period times a million."

"It's too early for the baby, no?" Cross asks Doc, who doesn't look too happy with what he's hearing. But then again, he never looks particularly happy.

"It's gonna be fine," he says in his Southern drawl and I truly hope he's right, but I can't stay here right now.

"Where are you going?" Roxie calls after me shrilly, probably sure she'll never see me again. But she has no reason to be afraid.

"I'm going to find her," I say. "And then we'll come back."

Doc and Cross will take care of her now, she doesn't need me. But I think Barbie does, though probably not as much as I need her. I can't just let her go, and it's pointless trying to. Maybe I don't deserve her, maybe I'm no good for her, and maybe we'll have a fight on our hands so we can be together, but damn it, I'm good at fighting. I'll do everything I can to prevent what happened to my father and his MC from happening again. And I need Barbie by my side.

Whatever comes, we'll figure it out together. Like she wanted to. There's no figuring out anything without her anyway. I do love her, she wasn't wrong about that either. On the whole, it's mostly me who's been wrong about a lot of things lately.

## 19

ICE

IT'S an hour's ride to the Saloon where I dropped Barbie off last night, but it feels like fucking days are passing before I reach it. The place looks pretty much deserted, with only a couple of bikes parked out front and no music coming from the inside, since it's so early in the day, but this is one of those places that are always open. I'm hoping Barbie just spent the night here. I mean, how fast can she find another guy? A fun and pretty girl like her, probably in less than an hour.

Something clicked in my head while Roxie shouted at me to get my life together, even while she was in pain and probably frightened that something was wrong with her baby. It finally drove home the point Barbie's been making all this time. There's always loss and hurt in life, there's no running away from it. And there's no sense in running away from the best thing that happened to me in the last seven years, maybe ever.

Barbie's it, and I was such a fucking idiot leaving her here. I hardly remember my reasons right now and I hope she forgives me. She might, it's only been just over twelve hours. But I better not find her in some other guy's lap, because he's not gonna know what hit him. I know full well I left her behind to do just that, but I won't remember that technicality when I see it. She's mine.

Inside, a couple of guys are passed out, slumped over their tables, and the only woman here is the waitress. She's half asleep behind the bar, but perks up when I walk up to her.

"Do you remember the woman who was with me last night?" I ask. I can tell she knows who I am, most bikers and their hangers-on do, since I'm famous as the six-year running Death Match champion. Guys wanna fight me now, and women want to fuck me. I think this one does too, but it's hard to tell since she can't open her eyes fully.

"She followed you outside, I thought she left

with you," the waitress says, looking puzzled, but then she grins. "And neither of you paid for the drinks."

I toss a twenty on the counter. "She didn't come back in afterwards? Think."

"I don't gotta think," she says, still smiling at me. "I was kinda hoping you'd both come back in."

She glides her hand over my forearm, but I barely feel it.

"I gotta find her. If she comes in, tell her I was here looking for her," I say, ignoring her hand on my arm. "You know who I am, right?"

"Yes," she says and gives me another winning smile. "You're Iceman the Champion. I hoped to get to know you better last night. But you can stay now, can't you? She might come back, so why not just wait for her here?"

A couple of months ago, I might've found her talking to me like this flattering. I might've even taken her in the back and given her what she clearly wants, but now, now the memory of every woman I've ever been with before Barbie is faded and boring.

I have to find her, but I have no idea where to begin. For a while, I figured I at least got being the champion to show for my life. But now, even that pales in comparison to the life I could have with

Barbie, if I didn't make such a mess of it last night. I hope it's not too late to fix it.

"Tell her Ice is looking for her and to stay put if she comes back here," I say. "I'll be back later."

She groans disappointedly, but I'm already halfway to the door.

I hope Barbie didn't get lost in the woods last night. But she's a smart woman who's been on her own for a long time. I fucked up so bad last night and of all my mistakes, this one burns the hottest. I need to find a way to fix it.

After an hour of walking through the woods and calling out her name, I know it's pointless. Birds are singing, wood is creaking, the wind is rustling the branches, and from time to time I hear a bike roar past on the road. The rest of the time it's peaceful and serene, and she's not answering my calls.

I doubt even Hawk can find her for me, she's the kind of girl who doesn't leave a huge footprint. Except the one she left on my heart, that one is deep and huge. So Hawk better find her.

---

BARBIE

I DIDN'T SLEEP LONG, the noon day sun woke me by shining bright and hot right in my eyes. Not the best way to wake up and on top of my eyes watering now, I'm also starving and aching all over from my all-night hike. But my heart still hurts worst of all. And if all that wasn't uncomfortable enough, what I thought was the ocean at dawn is actually just a huge blue tarp covering something large in the distance. Figures, because that's just my rotten luck in life.

It doesn't help knowing that all this is exactly what I should've expected either. I've had my heart broken more times than I can count, it's the story of my life, but I just keep giving it away like some damn idiot who never learns. Ice broke it worst of all, because he showed me everything I wanted, held it out for me to take and hold and get used to. And then he snatched it right back and left me on the side of the road like a piece of trash.

Maybe that's all I am. Maybe I should finally accept it. This world has proven it to me over and over and over again. I'm not meant to be loved.

But I can have fun.

It's the same conclusion I always come to, and it's always worked for me, and always helps get me moving. Yet today, my legs feel like they're stuck in blocks of concrete as I walk back to the road I passed to get to the top of the hill last night. I'll hitch a ride with the first bikers that pass, just like I've always done.

By the time I reach the road, I still don't think this is a good idea. But Ice doesn't want me. Even though I know he does. Which still makes no sense, but it is as it is. And where else can I go? The world of bikers is all I know, it's my home, and if I stay in it, then Ice can find me that much easier when he comes to his senses.

The asphalt has already absorbed enough of the day's heat to give it off, and I feel very alone as I sit by the side of the road waiting for someone to drive by. No one does. Not for a very long time.

Then I hear the roaring of bikes in the distance and my hearts starts skipping beats, butterflies fluttering in my stomach as my chest fills with excitement of a new adventure on the horizon. And all that's just because my stupid mind hopes it's Ice coming back for me.

But it can't be, I walked for miles last night, he has no idea where to look for me. I'll just hitch a ride with whoever it is, I'm good at getting rides. I'll do just like he told me to do. Let's see how he likes it. He won't like it one bit, I'm sure of that.

Then I'll stick around these parts for him to come and find me. I won't fuck anyone else until he comes back for me. If I can help it, though I might not get a choice, since most guys aren't like him, aren't kind and considerate like him. They just take what they want. I wish he wanted me bad enough to just take me forever. But I'm sure it won't take long for him to come back for me, because I don't think he can stay away. Not if that kiss and hug last night is anything to go by. And if he doesn't come back? Well, this life is all I have, no matter how many times it breaks my heart, that's still true. It's where I belong.

I step out into the middle of the road once the sound of bikes grows louder, smiling and waving my arms. I'm good at moving on, I'm a pro at it, it's all I've ever done.

The bikes encircle me from all sides and only then stop. One glance at their backs and my heart starts beating to a completely different tune. Fear and terror and just plain old disappointment. I wish I'd just stayed hidden, just stayed lost in the woods forever. Fuck my luck. Or no, scratch that, because I have none anyway.

"Hello, Barbie!" Brick yells out, already getting off his bike. "Fancy meeting you here. What a stroke of luck."

Yeah, this piece of shit bastard has all the luck, always had. I never could understand how assholes like him could always be so lucky, but here it is. I can't run away, his crew would stop me, probably violently, so I don't even try.

"What are you doing out here all alone?" he asks as he stops in front of me.

"I was just taking a walk," I say and smile at him. But his punch, the one I've been anticipating since he took off his helmet, isn't any gentler despite that effort. I'm on my hands and knees, fighting to stay conscious and hoping he doesn't have a kick coming my way too.

"You and your walks, Barbie," he says as he grabs me by the arm and hoists me back to my feet roughly. I'm seeing two of him, where one is already too much, and I'm not even entirely sure my name is Barbie.

"Can I take her now?" Razor's slimy voice reminds me of everything I'd prefer to forget.

Brick pushes me towards him. "Yeah, she's all yours. Though I wouldn't mind teaching her a thing or two about respect, but I'll leave that to you. Let's ride. The sooner we get out of these parts, the better."

"You really are the luckiest man on earth," Razor tells him as he drags me towards his bike. "We didn't even have to go through the Devils to get her back."

Brick laughs his harsh old man laugh and says something, but I don't even hear it. Yeah, he's the luckiest son of a bitch alive, and I'm right back where I started this adventure.

But maybe I'll be able to run away once we get back on the road. At some traffic stop or something, the sooner the better. I'll just jump off the bike and raise hell until they decide it's safer to just leave me be.

That chance could be a long time coming though, because Razor has just tied my wrists together with his belt so tight, it's already cutting off the blood flow to my hands. He fixes the ends of the belt to the rails at the back of the seat.

"That's just so you don't fall off and disappear again," he tells me, and if I could, I'd kick him in the balls just to share some of this pain I'm in. Though I'd probably be in even more pain after that.

I have no idea how I'll ever get out of this, and that tiny voice of my sadness in my head is already asking me, "Why bother?"

I already found my soul mate, my one true love, the man I've been searching for my whole life. And then I lost him. What else is there for me to find?

# 20

ICE

No one knows where Hawk is, and he's not answering his phone. He's my only hope of tracking down Barbie. I can't sit still and I don't know where else to look.

I've been to the Saloon twice already, and most of the clubhouses and bars around here, but she's nowhere. I almost got into five fights asking around for Barbie and I'm about to go to the Saloon again. This time, if she's still not there, I just might get into one of those fights. I've been avoiding them, because I can't risk getting incapacitated before I find her. I have to find her. I have to tell her how fucking wrong I was to leave her there last night, and how fucking sorry I am for not seeing that sooner.

I'm starting to understand I might never find her again. And that'll fucking never sit well with me.

"Hey, Ice, wait up," Rook yells after me from the front door of Sanctuary, then jogs to the garage where I'm getting on my bike.

"Hawk just checked in," he says. "He should be back soon."

I get back off my bike. "What's soon?"

Rook shrugs and pockets his phone. "He didn't say. Could be ten minutes, could be an hour."

I almost get on my bike and drive off to the Saloon, because I have no idea what to do with myself for the next hour.

"Call him back," I say. "I want to ask him something,"

Rook shrugs, pulls his phone back out and dials. But there's no answer.

"Hawk checks in when Hawk wants to," he tells me as he disconnects the call. "It's his way and we no longer question it. He's got his quirks, but he always gets the job done."

Yeah, I noticed that about the guy, and it's pissing me off something awful right now. If I was president around here, or the Sarge like Rook is, I'd keep a tighter ship, just like my father did. But I won't say it, because I'm not running shit around here, so it's not my place to get smart about it.

Rook's eyeing me like he thinks I got some quirks too, and I hope he stays quiet about it, because I'm in no mood to start discussing that with him.

Just as I think he's about to say something, I hear the sound of an engine approaching in the distance. We both look over at the driveway, and for the time it took the black truck to pull up, I was really hoping Rook was wrong about that one hour, and that it's Hawk returning.

Cross and Doc get out of the truck, neither of them looking very pleased.

"Where's Roxie?" I ask.

Nothing ever shows on Cross' face, but right now he looks pissed off as hell.

"She's alright. They're keeping her overnight but she's fine and the baby is fine too," Doc says, eying Cross out the side of his eyes like it's actually him he's talking to. "It was a false alarm."

"Yeah, but how do they know that?" Cross asks.

"They know," Doc assures him. "And it was best for us to get out of their way. You were making it hard for them to work and agitating her besides. Don't be so worried, she's in good hands."

He finishes that with a little chuckle, which turns Cross' gaze a few shades darker.

He turns to me. "Did you find the woman?"

I shake my head.

"What woman?" Rook asks. I haven't told him why I need to speak to Hawk. It was bad enough thinking I'd never see Barbie again all day without talking about it.

"That was a fool move, what you did," Cross says. "I told you as much. You both should've just stayed put with us here. Now Roxie's sick and worried, I don't know what the fuck to do with the Bloods and the Kings when they come knocking, and—"

"I said I'll deal with them," I interrupt, since it looks like he's just gonna keep listing all the ways in which I fucked all this up and, again, it's bad enough just thinking about it.

"Another fool move," Cross says. "I'd never let you meet them alone, if you were one of us."

That's another dumbass decision of mine.

These men have bled for me, they've laid their lives on the line so I could get my revenge. They're as close to brothers as I'll ever have again, and I owe them my life. Which I'd gladly lay down for any of them to repay them for all they've already done for me. Yet I keep fighting that fact too. Why? So I can continue being alone in my head with my dark thoughts that are tearing me apart worse now than they did back when I was still in Lizard's cell?

"I would like to join your club, if you'll still have me," I say and it makes whatever Cross was gearing up to say stick in his throat.

"You've all laid down your lives for me, and the only way I can ever hope to repay that is by doing the same for you. Brothers." The word sticks in my throat, and it does bring a wave of ice cold over my chest, but I think it's the last one of those. Because now that the word is out there, it fucking feels great.

They all kinda froze when I said it, even Cross, but he nods thoughtfully then extends his hand to me. "Brothers."

I shake on it and Rook laughs out loud and smacks me on the back. "Fucking finally, man."

"What kinda bonding moment did I miss?" Tank yells as he strides towards us from the house.

"I asked to join up," I tell him, which wipes that sarcastic grin right off his face. He even slows down a little bit.

"And I accepted," Cross adds.

Tank opens his mouth to speak then closes them again, and repeats it a couple of times with no sound coming out. This is the first time since I've known him that he hasn't had a sarcastic comment or two ready to go.

"What, cat got your tongue, Tank?" Rook says, probably noticing the same thing.

Tank just shakes his head and gives me a big old pat on the back. "Nah, I'm just happy you finally came around, Ice. No point being the lone wolf when a whole new pack wants to adopt you, am I right?"

"I see you and Cross spoke about this," I say, since this is pretty much the same thing as what Cross said to me last night. "But yeah, I was a fool to try and stay away. My old brothers are dead and buried. But a man can have more brothers."

"Nicely put," Tank says and gives me another smack on the back. "I'd add that I hope your butchering days are behind you, but then again, to each his own."

They all look at me sharply as he says it, and I would expect a more striking memory of slicing open a Spawn to come up in my head from his words, but it doesn't. Maybe the time to close that chapter has finally caught up to me too.

"They're behind me," I assure them. And I'd say more, but the sound of bikes approaching wipes it straight from my mind.

Hawk's back.

"What are you all doing out here?" he asks as he gets off his bike. "Taking a romantic evening stroll together?"

Rook winces, but Tank grins. "Yeah, and you're

not invited, if all you're gonna do is mock," he says, since he always has some smartass comment ready to throw.

Hawk grins back. "Alright, that's enough of trying to be funny. Since you're all here, I might as well tell you what I found out now. I've been to damn near every bar and rest stop from here to too far away, but I tracked those bastards down."

My heart's beating so fast it's about to thump it's way right out of my chest.

"As for the even better news, one of my informants, a tough old broad named Lucy, just called me, and she's pretty sure they found that woman of theirs and are heading back to Illinois. So it looks like our problem took care of itself."

"What else did this Lucy say?" I hear myself ask, but my voice sounds like it's coming from very far away.

Hawk glances at me then narrows his eyes at Cross, like he's asking him if he should answer. Cross nods.

"Lucy also said the woman didn't look too pleased to be there. She's bruised up and tied up, but docile enough. Lucy doesn't want to get involved, and asked us not to come there to smash up her place either. But I don't know, I guess it's your decision."

I don't know if he's talking to me or Cross, but it doesn't matter. I've already made my decision. My heart's not beating anymore, and I'm frozen so stiff I shouldn't be able to move. But I will be. I know this zone, I entered it before every fight, and it only allows one thought into my brain—win. Later, I entered it before killing every Spawn that I could. I'm back in that zone now, and there's still no room for any other thought. I will win Barbie back.

"Where are they?" I ask.

"This shitty place called the Rusty Bucket just off Route 90," Hawk says, eyeing me very closely.

I'm on my bike without realizing I've moved.

"No, Ice," Cross says. "We do this together. That's an order."

"You want the woman back?" Tank asks, looking from me to Cross and back. "I thought you sent her packing."

"That was a mistake I made," I say, practically praying it doesn't turn out to be the worst one I've ever made. Joining the Devils might've been a mistake too, if Cross is gonna stop me from going after Barbie now.

"How many guys do they have?" Cross asks Hawk.

"About thirty, she says," Hawk tells us. "And

another thirty kept riding when the ones with the woman stopped. Lucy was real happy about that."

"Alright, we'll take fifty and ride," Cross says.

I expected I'd have to argue to get him to say this, and I still got some of those arguments hammering away in my brain. Now that I've called these men brothers, I don't want them to risk their lives for me that much more. But now that I've called them brothers, that kinda logic doesn't make a whole lotta sense to me anymore either. This is how it is between brothers. They got my back and I got theirs. To the end. It's the rule that stands above all other rules. And I'll gladly follow it.

"Thank you," I say because it's the only thing that makes sense to say.

"You're one of us now, Ice," he replies.

"Alright, let's go get that lady love of yours back," Rook says. "I've been itching to repay that particular favor to you."

He's referring to the time I helped him get his own lady love back in Mexico.

"There's no need to repay me for anything, but I'd appreciate your help," I tell him.

It comes out kinda cold, because I'm back in that state in which I never lose. And I hope to Christ this is the last time I'll have to visit it. Because I'm less than human when I'm in here, I'm an animal that cares about nothing except getting what I'm after. But this will be the most important fight of my life. Because Barbie has to live, and all my brothers need to live, and I've got to live too.

---

BARBIE

WE RODE all day after they found me on the road. Or more precisely, after I ran right into their nasty paws. Now, we stopped at a seedy restaurant in the middle of nowhere. Brick's grinning at me from over by the bar like he's enjoying seeing me tied up and treated like dirt, like the last five years we spent together never happened. Twilight has fallen outside, and I can't feel my hands anymore. It's all putting me in an even fouler and blacker mood than I was already in, and just keeps getting worse.

Razor led me inside by the belt still tied around my wrists, which a lot of the guys found real entertaining. I don't think I've ever gotten my ass smacked and my boobs and pussy groped as many times as I did in the short walk from Razor's bike to this table where he proceeded to tie my hands to the legs of it, grinning that black-toothed smile of his all the while.

I get where Ice was coming from now in a way I couldn't before, because I've never had my freedom taken away completely, never been seen as just a thing, just a piece of property for them to do as they like with. Oh God, I hope Razor doesn't give me to these hyenas of his for a some gang rape action before we move on from here, but I wouldn't put it past him. Maybe that's all my future with him will be—random beatings and the humiliation of letting his men do what they want with me. He didn't stop the groping, and he's not stopping the leering and the foul comments now. That's a pretty bad sign right there. And I hope even more that he doesn't decide to fuck me before we ride off again. But he's an old guy, he probably can't get it up that well anymore. Just like Brick couldn't.

Fuck Ice for just leaving me at the side of the road! But I get it. Just half a day of this captivity shit, and I'm ready to throw in the towel. I'd never survive six years of it like he did.

"Here's your dinner," Razor says, dumping a plate of baked beans and potatoes on the table in front of me, spilling about a third of it.

"How you expect me to eat this?" I snap and show

him my tied hands. "Why don't you just put in on the floor, and I'll eat it like a dog."

I should be making nice with him, should be trying to make him fall in love with me. Then he'd untie me, and I could run away. But I hate him so much, I hate them all so much, the only one I want is Ice, and he's never coming back for me, so I don't even care what happens now. That's just some more of my stupid thinking though.

Hanging all my hopes on men got me into this mess I'm in now, and I know that perfectly well, I figured it out while I walked all night. But, damn it, it's how I feel, and I was never good at fighting my feelings. So, yeah, I don't care what happens now unless it's Ice coming in through that door to tell me he's sorry for leaving me.

And I kinda think that's gonna happen any moment now, but what actually happens is, I get a stinging, hard backhanded smack across my face. It leaves me with the taste of blood in my mouth and the bells ringing in my head from the last punch getting even louder. But they're not louder than the shouts and laughter of approval from the other men in here. Brick is grinning at me complacently, and if I had any lingering hopes of getting some compassion from him, I see now how dead wrong I was.

"You wanna eat off the floor?" Razor asks, and

hurls the plate at the wall, causing it to snap in half and making the beans and potatoes fly everywhere. "Go eat then, you ungrateful bitch. I don't even gotta feed you, you know?"

He unties the belt from the table leg and yanks on it, causing me to fall to the floor along with the chair.

"What's going on here?" a woman asks sharply.

I look up at her, but her head is a long way up and I can hardly see her face. She's gotta be at least six feet tall, and she's all formidable looking, but I'm not entirely sure she stepped in to help me. She hardly even glanced at me. Razor's vicious grin is frozen on his face as he looks up at her too.

"I won't have this kinda behavior in here," the woman says. "You can take your business elsewhere."

The whole place is completely silent now, Razor's hoarse old man breathing the only sound I can hear.

"Get out of my joint," she repeats herself. "We like it real nice and peaceful in here, and I'm gonna keep it that way."

I can see some of the guys stirring and reaching for their guns, but they all know the same thing I know. She wouldn't be making a stand like this unless she could back it up. And I know Brick and Razor don't want any trouble. They're too far away from home, and more than half of their men kept riding when we stopped here.

"Let's get outta here, Razor," Brick yells. "The food's terrible and the service even worse."

He could always be counted on to be the first one making a cowardly decision.

The lady doesn't even bat an eye as Razor yanks me to my feet by the belt, the force of his pull breaking skin. I'm sad to find out I was right about her. She didn't do this to help me, that's none of her business, she did it for exactly the reason she gave— to keep things nice and peaceful in her joint.

At least the guys aren't rowdy and gropey as we file out. And at least the threat of getting gang raped isn't hanging right over my head anymore for the time being. But God damn it, everything is still as black and bleak as it was when we walked in here. Blacker and bleaker even, because we're about to ride out even further away from where Ice might be looking for me.

Fuck Ice for just leaving me. Fuck me for returning right back to the place I've been trying to flee since I found it. Fuck my luck and my life. I've always been good at finding the silver lining in everything, but there is none in this, and that's possibly the scariest of all the things I'm facing right now.

## 21

ICE

HAWK RODE on ahead to check the situation at the Rusty Bucket, and he's standing next to a huge woman under the awning in front of the door as we approach.

"They already left," Hawk tells us completely unnecessarily since that's obvious from the lack of other bikes in the lot.

The woman next to him has her arms crossed over her large breasts and the look on her face clearly says, *no one better mess with me*.

"How long ago?" I ask her.

"Half an hour, maybe less. Don't know exactly,

since I've been cleaning up the mess they left and lost track of the time," she tells me. "Good riddance, I say, they were making too much noise, and I didn't like the way they were treating that woman they had with them. I didn't want anything to happen to her on my doorstep."

If my blood was running cold before, it's frozen now. She didn't want anything to happen to Barbie here, but she couldn't care less if it happens somewhere else is what she's actually saying. I don't call her out on it though, since it's all my fault in the first place, and there's no time for chitchat, so I stay quiet and head for my bike.

"Which way did they go?" Cross asks and she points at the road leading past this place to the east.

"You're a good woman, Lucy," Hawk tells her. "We'll get the bastards who messed up your fine establishment."

"That's enough talking, Hawk," I yell out, already sitting on my bike. I have no business talking to him like this, and his harsh, dirty look tells me as much, but there's no time for that either.

"We going or what?" I ask Cross.

He exchanges a look with Tank, Rook and Scar, who also joined us for this ride.

"A road takedown," Tank muses. "It's been awhile since we've done one of those."

He doesn't exactly sound like he's against it, but that's what I'm hearing anyway.

"What, you scared you've gotten too old?" Scar snaps at him. I'd never speak to my VP that way, since hierarchy must always be observed on jobs. My father taught me that, but Scar has no problem with it, and it works in my favor now.

"Man, we're the same age," Tank says indignantly, but he's grinning, probably because Scar's well known for saving damsels in distress no matter the cost.

"Alright, enough of that," Cross says. "We're gonna do this, and we ain't got much time."

I was grateful to him before, but hearing him say that takes it to a whole new level.

"We overtake them and make them stop," he continues. "Then we get the woman back peaceful-like. That's the plan, so no one fucking be brave, is that clear?"

He's looking at me as he says it, and I nod, but the truth is, I'm gonna do whatever it takes to get Barbie away from them.

"I'm gonna need you to take my lead on this one, Ice," Cross says, probably picking up on me thinking that. "That means you hide your face and let me do the talking. It's dark and they probably won't see you coming, but I'm not gonna take the risk. I want them to think we're just a random group of bikers taking them over on the road until it's too late for them."

I reach into my pocket for the bandana they gave me a long time ago, and which I've refused to wear on any of the Spawn's killings, since I wanted them to see me coming. The half heart pendant almost falls out with it, but I catch it and hang it around my neck where it belongs, before tying the bandana over my face like the rest of them have already done.

"Alright, Prez," I say.

I want Barbie to see my face when I come for her, I want her to see me from far away, but this is bigger than just me, and Cross' plan is better.

"Let's ride!" Cross calls out and drives off, taking the lead.

I'm right beside him at the front of the column, and we're riding so fast the cold wind is ripping up my face despite the bandana I'm wearing. The feeling coursing through my veins is just as intense as it was that night when I chased the taillights of the men who killed my father and burned down his house. But on that night I was chasing death, whereas tonight I'm chasing life. The only life I want, and, damn it, I want to live it.

As the red lights of the bikes we're chasing finally come into view, my blood's not frozen anymore, it's flowing hot, burning like fire. I'm still focused on one thing, and one thing only—winning. This is not a fight I can lose, and I know that with everything that I am.

---

WE'RE ALMOST ON THEM. I can already see Barbie's blonde hair flapping in the wind behind her. She's trying to turn and look back, but can't manage it very well, because she's sitting weirdly on the back of the bike of what I think is the guy she was being given to when I stopped it. Her hands are bound behind her back so tight her shoulders are pulled all the way back, and he's gonna fucking pay for causing her that pain too, separately from paying for everything else.

Cross is waving to me to fall back, then sends a group of guys behind us forward. The Devils have a thousand and one hand gestures, something for signaling anything that might come up in a job. I've only learned the most basic ones, and usually ignored those too during the jobs they took me on, but I guess I'll have to learn the rest now that I'm one of them. They're like a well-oiled engine when it comes to carrying out jobs, each member doing their part perfectly and efficiently. That's the reason they can't lose, which is something I learned early on.

Ahead, the assholes who took Barbie aren't stopping, they're just getting out of the way so our guys can pass them. I can't see Barbie anymore, and the combined sound of all our bikes—more than eighty hogs going full speed down a two-lane country road —sounds like a jet plane taking off. Or crashing. I'm out of patience. I need to reach her, I need to get her off that guy's bike and on the back of mine where she belongs.

Cross gives an angry, cutting gesture when I gun it to pass him, and I don't need to know exactly what it means to know what he's saying. *My way. Back off.* So I slow down again.

A few moments later the group in front of us finally starts slowing down. They're completely stopped by the time me and Cross reach them.

"What's the meaning of this?" that old boyfriend of Barbie's yells in the sudden silence, which is still carrying the echoes of rumbling bikes.

"We've come to take the woman back!" I yell and rip off my bandana in the split second before Barbie turns her head to me. The gratitude in her face— which is all banged up again, God damn it—renders me speechless and breathless. There's love in her eyes, along with happiness and relief, and maybe some anger too, which is the one thing out of all the rest that I really deserve.

"You came back for me," she says, and it's little more than a whisper, but I hear it loud and clear.

"I was an idiot for leaving you, Barbie. I'm sorry," I tell her loud enough for everyone to hear. But I don't care about that. It's like we're the only ones here anyway.

"Yeah, you were," she says. "But you're starting to make up for it."

She's not wrong. I'm only just starting to do that and we should get a move on finishing it, so me and her can be alone together for real. There's eighty bikers around us, most of them already setting up for a fight.

"You heard him!" Cross yells. "Let's do this nice and friendly-like, so no one gets hurt. You're surrounded, and Devil's Nightmare MC has no problem leaving you all dead on this lonely stretch of road far from home. But you already knew that."

The mention of what club they're dealing with has the desired effect, and most of the guys reaching for their guns freeze.

"You rode for a woman?" Brick asks mockingly. "I've heard talk that you were going soft, Cross, but this is kinda a new low, don't you think?"

"Don't taunt me, Brick," Cross replies, nothing in his voice saying Brick's words had any effect on him at all, but it sure suggests he's gonna stop the taunts if he has too. Swiftly and completely. "And don't try to test me, either. You're outnumbered, and at least twenty years too late to win this fight."

That makes lots of guys laugh, but the longer this takes, the longer Barbie's not in my arms. She's not laughing, and the look she's giving me is saying more than just how happy she is to see me. It also tells me to be wary of that guy, and she knows him better than anyone. I'm not worried about Cross and the guys handling this, because I know they will. I'm just worried about all the stray bullets that could start flying before it gets handled. She's tied down and she's not next to me where I could take those bullets instead of her.

"Alright, just give her to them," Brick says, probably surprising everyone, and certainly surprising Barbie. She shoots him such a puzzled gaze, there's no doubt in my mind that he's full of shit.

"She ain't worth dying over," he adds. *Oh, yeah, she is.*

"She ain't yours to give," the guy whose bike she's on yells. "And I ain't giving her up without a fight."

He revs his bike and speeds up directly into the line of my brothers blocking their path. All hell breaks loose, as he does it, bikes roaring to life, men yelling, shots ringing out.

But all I see is Barbie's eyes as she looks at me

from the back of the guy's bike. Her eyes don't need any light to be as bright blue as the calmest ocean. And I don't need anything other than to look into her eyes.

I gun it, reach them before they reach the line of my brothers. I'm almost close enough to touch her hand, but the guy just keeps speeding on.

"Move the fuck out of the way, I got this!" I yell at the brothers blocking his path while signaling it at the same time.

They part, the guy aims for the hole, and I'm right beside him as he makes it through the barrier.

I reach out to grab her arm, but Barbie shouts something I can't hear and wriggles her bound hands to show me she's completely tied down to the bike.

I have my knife out in a flash, the knife I couldn't stop touching, let alone throw away even after I no longer had any use for it. And this is why I couldn't bury it in my father's grave. The knife I used to avenge my family had this one last job to do. Free Barbie so she could be mine forever. It's the most important job it ever had.

However, actually getting up close enough to cut the belt she's tied down with is another matter. The old guy keeps flashing me looks over his shoulder, as he rides faster than he's ridden in the last thirty years by the looks of him. We've left the fight behind and he knows it. He probably already knows he's beaten too. But he ain't backing down. Yet this is not a fight I'll lose.

I level my bike with the end of his for another try to free Barbie, and she pulls the belt as taut as she can, needing no prompting to help me out, just like she never once did from the moment we met.

This time I manage to cut the belt. I toss the knife away the second her hands are free, because I need my right hand to hoist her off his bike and into my lap. She grabs my arm tight and slides to me through the air like she's done this a thousand times before, just as seamlessly and perfectly as she followed me out the bar on that first night we met. I don't think it's because she's practiced at this. I just think it's because we're so perfectly in synch. We're a team, always were, she was right about that too.

Her lips are less than an inch from mine and all I want to do is kiss her, because, frankly, I've never been happier than when I'm holding her in my arms and kissing her, and just that will always be enough for me. But there's no time for that yet. If I wanna keep holding her I gotta get us out of this first.

The old guy hit the brakes once he realized she wasn't on his bike anymore, but he tried to turn with too much speed. He screamed as his bike slipped, and he's still groaning now that he's buried beneath it. He's writhing as he tries to get out from under it, but a split second later it becomes clear that's not what he was doing. I'm staring down the barrel of a colt shining a cold silver in the moonlight.

I faced a gun like this in the middle of an empty road on a dark night once before. And for seven years after that, I fucking wished with all that was left of my heart and my mind that I'd taken a bullet from that gun on that night. But now, as the gun fires and the bullet flies towards us, that is my worst fear.

I push Barbie down and shelter her with my body, and veer so hard to the left we almost go down too. My back's turned to the bullet now and I'm expecting it to hit any second. But at least she'll live, the muscles I've built while I was Lizard's prisoner will stop it before it reaches her. The bullet reaches us. And misses. It flies out into the night and disappears.

Not so the one that comes back from the darkness. But this one misses us by a good couple of feet and hits the guy squarely between the eyes.

"We're even now, man," Rook tells me as he pulls up beside us, holstering his gun.

Tank and Scar are right behind him, with Doc riding towards us too.

"Where's the rest of them?" I ask as I straighten up, releasing Barbie from the tight hold I had on her.

She's shivering in my arms, and I'm still holding her so tight my arm hurts. But I gotta know we're safe, before I give her all my attention.

"They're subdued," Tank says. "Cross is talking to them."

"Anyone down?" I ask, my voice hollow.

"No, we're all good," Rook assures me, laughing right after.

And that's all I needed to know.

Barbie's electric blue eyes are like two lasers pointing right at my heart as I loosen my grip on her and look into her face.

"I'm so sorry, babe," I tell her. "I wasn't thinking straight when I left you."

"Yeah, I told you so," she says. "But you wouldn't listen."

"I should've listened," I say. "I love you with all my heart too, Barbie."

I don't care that we're surrounded by guys probably thinking what I just said to her is best done in private. But I want the whole world to know this, and I want her to know it most of all.

"I know you do," she whispers, but her eyes are flooded now, the sea they look like wavy and shimmering.

I kiss her despite the bloody cut on her lip that's all my fault, and she kisses me back, and all is as right with the world as it ever was, as it ever can be. The road, the night, the brothers, it all fades away while we kiss. The world is ours again. We're alone on that beach I promised to take her to, but didn't, we're alone by the fire at the lake washed in moonlight, we're alone in the motel room, her naked body bathed in orange from the streetlight outside our window. And the best part is, now we can do all that all over again. Nothing and no one matters more than her.

"Ice?" Doc says with a chuckle. "Let me get a look at her cuts and such."

His words make me realize I'm tasting blood and it's not my own. It's also enough to make me realize I'm probably hurting her by holding her this tight, and kissing her this hard. But maybe not, since she's very reluctant to let me go once I start to pull away.

"Let him look you over," I tell her, then get off my bike with her in my arms and sit her down on it.

She nods and lets him get to work, only winces and sighs a little as he cleans her cuts, and wraps her wrists where the belt dug into them. I feel all that pain as though it's my own. Because all those cuts and bruises are my fault. But I'll never let her suffer another one for as long as I live.

"You should take her home for some rest now," Doc tells me once he's done tending to her, but she looks at me and smiles.

"I'll be just fine, and he promised to take me to the ocean," she says and I can't help smiling too.

"And a promise is a promise," I tell her. "Let's do it."

She nods, gets off my bike so I can get on, then climbs on behind me, all as smooth and seamless as anything else we do together.

I drive off, and I wouldn't stop until we reach the ocean, but Cross has all the guys who tried to take her kneeling in the middle of the road, and I'm thinking maybe Barbie wants to say goodbye to Brick once and for all.

"What's gonna happen to them?" she asks as she gets off the bike. There's no emotion in her voice, and her eyes are alike two blue marbles, hard and reflective.

She's talking to me, but Cross answers. "We're gonna let them go, since we got what we came for. So if you have any last words to say to them, now's your chance."

She pulls me along by my hand as she walks up to Brick who's also kneeling on the pavement with his hands clasped behind his back. Her steps are measured and firm, but a storm is brewing in her marble-hard eyes.

"You messed up real bad trying to trade me in, Brick, and I hope you know it now," she tells him. "I never want to see you again, but I do want to give you a parting gift."

She doesn't miss a beat as she kicks him right in the nose. He yells out and keeps yelling as his hands fly to his face and dark blood starts oozing from between his fingers. She has gorgeous, smooth legs, but they're hella strong too. I know that, and I can't wait to have them wrapped around me again.

"We'll take that as you two officially being broken up," Cross tells him, trying to suppress a laugh. "No more talk of this being your woman, is that clear?"

Brick nods, his eyes spewing black venom in Barbie's direction.

"No, no more talk of that. She's my woman," I say and get a very tight hug, along with a very lovely look and bright smile as my thanks.

"Yes, and that means she's ours too," Cross adds. "So think about that first, if you ever get the itch to ride out West again."

It's my turn to give a grateful look and Cross just nods at me.

"Now let's wrap this up," he says.

Me and Barbie are the first to reach our bike. I

can't wait to get on the road again, so it can once again be just me and her, alone together, with the rumbling of my bike filling my ears, the warm wind in my face and her soft body pressed against my back. For the first time in seven years, I'm truly looking forward to traveling the road ahead of me.

## 22

Barbie

My hope of ever getting away from Razor alive and whole was less substantial than a high summer breeze when I heard those other bikes closing in on us. But the very next second a calm and beautiful voice told me to hope hard. That my shit life was about to end once and for all in the best way possible.

Then I heard him call my name and saw his face and I knew the voice was telling me the truth.

Ice came after me. Against all hope, against all that seemed impossible, he found me and he saved me, and right now, as I sit beside him in the warm sand watching the sun rise over the ocean, memories of my shit life before we met are already fading like a bad nightmare.

He's wearing the other half of the necklace I forced him to take that night when he wouldn't tell me he loved me. I saw it gleaming in the moonlight as he snatched me off Razor's bike and saved me for the second time. I didn't even need to hear him say, "I love you", after that. I already knew it. But it felt amazing hearing it too.

We rode all night to get here.

He wanted to stop and let me rest, but I insisted we keep going. I don't need rest, I just need him. I need him holding me just like this, letting me lean on him, I need him keeping his promises to me, and I need him loving me. Because he's the one I've been searching for my whole life and I've finally found him.

"I didn't think you'd come after me," I say and press even closer to him. "I hoped you would, sure, I hoped for that very much, but I didn't think it was possible. I guess you coming after me just proves my point some more, though."

He wraps his arm around my shoulders tighter and pulls me even closer, chuckling. "And which point is that, Barbie?"

He's referring to the fact that I talk a lot. And I do.

"The point that me and you were destined to find each other. We were meant to meet when I first came to your town, but you had just left," I tell him. "It was fate then, we just got interrupted. But it was always fate, so we got another chance now."

The first time I told him this it annoyed him, though that was before he told me he loved me. But I'm still kinda expecting a similar response now, which doesn't matter, because I know it's the truth.

"You might be right, who knows?" he says instead. "But what I do know is that from the moment I saw you, I knew you were the one for me. It just took me a long time to catch up to that knowing."

"Better late than never," I say, and that's the truth too.

"And speaking of doing the impossible, you did that for me too," he says. "I was sure I'd never love anything or anyone again, and that I'd never have a family again. Hell, I even figured I wouldn't live much longer."

I gasp and look at him in shock, because he sounded so cold and my heart started racing in absolute terror when he mentioned dying. But his eyes are showing me glorious spring as he smiles and grips me even tighter.

"You changed all that," he says. "And now I hope to live to a ripe old age. With you by my side."

"Good," I whisper, getting lost in his eyes, which are showing me nothing but love and truth and devotion that's beyond anything mere words can do justice to.

"I wish I realized all that before. Then things would've played out differently," he adds.

"How so?" I ask, but I already know it from that gleam in his eyes. He wants me like no man has ever wanted me before, and he could never hide that from me, not even when he was being all quiet and standoffish in the beginning. Maybe that's why I knew right from the start that we were meant to be together.

"Well, for one thing, your face wouldn't be all banged up again and we could do more than sit here and hold each other," he says with a wide grin on his face.

"We can do more than sit here," I say and smile seductively, though I don't know if that's how it looks with all the cuts and bruises on my face.

But his soft warm eyes are telling me it looks just fine, just perfect. And I'm not just saying it either, I already hardly feel any pain, and it would go away completely if he kissed me and laid me down on this sand then took me like only he can.

He just smiles wider and kisses the top of my head instead of my lips "We've got plenty of time for that. This is nice too."

And he's not wrong about that. This is just about as perfect as things can get.

"What's next for us?" I ask.

"Once you're done looking at the ocean, I'll take you home," he says like it's the most logical thing in the world. "And then we'll see. We can pretty much do anything we want now."

"I like the sound of that," I say and lean against him again, my eyes closing, since I am sleepy, but I want to stay awake.

"But before all that, we could go get me that matching tattoo you wanted me to get," he says and I'm suddenly not sleepy at all anymore.

"You know, the missing part of your heart?" he adds, since maybe my whole body melting in sweet love and utter surprise that he remembered this one little thing must be making my face look like I have no idea what he's talking about.

But I know exactly what tattoo he's talking about. And I don't know what it feels like to get proposed to by the love of your life, but I'm sure this is better.

Sleep is the last thing on my mind, and my heart is racing again, but to a happy beat this time.

"Let's go do that right now," I say and move out of his arms, then think better of it as soon as our faces are level.

I kiss him instead of standing up, and nothing compares to that kiss. Not all the stars in the night sky, not the most gorgeous sunrises all happening at once, not thousands of butterflies flapping their gorgeous wings around us at the same time. The sweetness of it, the rightness and belonging erase all pain, past, present and future too.

And it gets even better as his hands slide under my shirt pushing it up as they do. The touch of his skin against my skin is electric, and I'm already tugging up his t-shirt so I can feel more of it. By then we both know where this is heading, and he does nothing to try and stop that runaway train of our passion from pulling into the station.

He lays me down on my back in the soft sand, kissing his way down my neck, only pausing long enough to remove my bra when his lips reach it. Then his lips are on my nipples, and the soft flesh of my breasts, my neck and my stomach, and his kisses feel like thousands of butterflies are landing on my naked skin, caressing me with their delicate wings.

Before I know it, I'm completely naked, his

butterfly kisses travelling down my legs and back up again. If I had any last doubts that he loves every single inch of me, they're completely erased once his lips find mine again, as his warm cock pulses against my clit.

He gives it to me slowly, staring deep into my eyes, my face reflected perfectly amid all the wild spring beauty in his. My moan is as never ending as the pleasure he's giving me. I want more, I want it all, but he pulls out and starts entering me again.

He does that again and again, until my moan becomes interlaced with gasps and whimpers as the sea inside me sends ever bigger waves of pleasure and bliss through my blood into every last part of my body.

The butterflies are within me now, caressing me from the inside as they did on the outside before. I feel like a virgin taken by the man of her dreams for the first time, and that's not just a wish right now, it's a fact, it's pure truth. I was a virgin until I gave myself to him, until he took me, because no one, absolutely no one, can make love to me in the perfect way he does, the way he's doing right now, the way he always will.

And I need more.

So I grip his hips and pull him closer, let more of him into me. He groans as I whimper, picking up his pace, entering me deeper, because this love we share, this passion we have for each other, this need of ours to be one, is out of our hands. It's fate. It's destiny and it's divine.

The waves of pleasure overflow inside me once he's buried in me all the way, filling me with his seed, giving me his orgasm, as I give him mine.

This is how it was always meant to be and now it finally can be. The time we spent apart, all those long years we searched for each other in vain are already melting away into nothing.

Me and him kissing and making love is fate, and there is no one and nothing that will convince me otherwise. My heart and my soul are his and his are mine. And that's how it will stay until we travel down the last road we're meant to ride. And beyond that too, I'm sure.

# EPILOGUE

*Two Years Later*

B<small>ARBIE</small>

I'VE BEEN STARING at the two grey lines for I don't know how long. It could be minutes, but it could also be hours. Maybe days. Years? It's not possible, at least I was sure it wasn't, but here it is, and this is the third test confirming it today.

The door to the suite Ice and me have been living in for the past two years opens and clicks shut. We thought about getting a house, but then decided to stay at Sanctuary. Roxie needed help with the baby and staying here made it easier to just take a ride whenever we felt like it. I've now seen all the oceans this land of ours is bordered with and some across the border too. And I've also seen everything in between. He showed it to me, along with so much else.

Besides, these rooms are nicer than any house I've ever seen. There's two of them, one the living room and the other our bedroom that's fit for a princess. And the bathroom is more beautiful than anything I've ever imagined. But we might have to get a house of our own now.

I'm so petrified of telling him, I'm frozen stiff. My hands aren't even shaking even though everything on the inside is. The last time I told a man this news, it didn't end well. It almost killed me.

"Barbie, you in here?" Ice yells from the living room. "I thought we could go grab dinner by the sea."

He likes going to the ocean as much as I do. It's our special thing. Sometimes we go sit on the beach and just watch the waves roll in for hours. We often make love in the sand too. Maybe we could get a house by the sea. But no, he has his work here and the ocean is a couple of hours away. And Roxie needs me here. Once me and her got to know each other better, we became the best of friends. We're two of a kind, her and I, and that just proves my point some more that me and Ice were meant to be.

I don't answer him, since just the walk from the bathroom to the bedroom is taking all the strength I can muster. I have my own means now, I'm a famous beauty and lifestyle youtuber and hundreds of thousands of women—women who used to look down their noses at me before—are now my biggest fans. I teach them to live their lives wild and free, and how to have fun. Hawk and Yana helped set me up, and Ice grumbles a lot about me talking to the camera for hours on end, but he's actually my biggest fan.

I could do this without him. But I don't want to!

He's undressing by the bed, half of him already naked and giving me the best view I've ever had the pleasure of laying my eyes on, or my hands, for that matter. I don't want to do anything without him!

"What's wrong?" he asks, probably reading my nervousness off my face, because he's really good at doing that. Unlike anyone else I know. That just proves my point some more, but this will be a big test.

"I...I'm...you're...You're gonna be a daddy," I finally stutter out, saying it like that, because it's a done deal. I hope it's a done deal.

He just stares at me, then stumbles a little before

plopping down on the bed. I have no idea what he's thinking right now, and I'm usually good at reading his face and his eyes too. At least it's not anger. At least he's not hitting me. But why would he? He never hits me. Why did I even fear he would now?

"You're not happy?" I ask, taking a few steps closer to him. Fear, that's mostly what's on his face.

"You think I'll make a good father?"

I know he's thinking back on all the darkness that was his life before we met, remembering all the vengeful death he witnessed and dealt out, and the cold, brooding, angry man all that changed him into. But I haven't seen much of that man in the last two years we've spent together. I've hardly seen that man at all.

I walk the rest of the way to the bed and sit down beside him, gripping his hand in both of mine. "You're the best man I know, and I can't imagine a better father."

I tell him that he's a good man from time to time, to remind him when he forgets, and that's not hard to do at all, because it's the complete and utter truth.

His eyes aren't as fearful anymore as they fix on mine, and they're not as unreadable anymore either. They're happy now and full of devotion. They're the eyes of the man I will love until the day I die, and probably beyond too.

"What is it? A boy or a girl?"

I laugh. "We can't know yet, silly. It's only been a couple of months...I think...maybe less. I hope it's a boy, personally."

"Why? It'd be nice to have a tiny version of you running around," he says. "And Hudson needs a little girl cousin to boss him around. Lily's not doing the best job of keeping him in check. They're too much alike."

I'm smiling, because I'm already picturing that whole scene in my head, and it's beautiful enough to make my eyes water.

"It's better to be a boy. It's easier," I say anyway. I always pictured my baby who died as a boy for precisely this reason.

He wipes away the tear that slipped from my eye with his thumb. "No daughter of mine's gonna have a hard time in life, I promise you that."

And I know he means it body and soul. He'll be her protector just like he's always been mine, and he won't ever think twice about loving her and keeping her safe.

"So you're happy?" I ask.

He kisses me instead of answering, making the birdsong coming in through the open window louder, making the scent of flowers grow stronger, and erasing all my fear and pain the way only his love can.

"I guess we might as well get married now too," he says once the kiss ends, then grins right after, probably in answer to my very wide and shocked eyes.

"That's the most unromantic proposal I've ever heard spoken, Brandon Knight," I say after gasping for effect.

He laughs. "Yeah, it probably is. The way I figure, it's just a ring and a name change, and with or without those two things, you already have all that's mine. But we might as well be thorough."

I shake my head in resignation, even though everything inside me is singing. "I'd love to have your name."

He kisses me again and doesn't stop just at my lips this time. I don't think we're gonna get to the ocean tonight. And if all he said didn't already convince me how happy he is with this news, his kisses are doing it now.

He starts undressing me and kisses every inch of my skin the moment it comes into view, some twice, some more often than that. I'm lighter than air, feel like a princess for real, as he lays me down on the cool sheets.

I'm his princess and he's my prince, and I'd gladly

live my whole life all over again, just so I could meet him again, just so I could fall in love with him all over again. Over and over again. For eternity.

*THE END*

—————

WANT TO READ ON? The next book in this series will be available soon! Sign up to receive an email alert the moment it is released by visiting http://www.lenabourne.com/devils-nightmare-series-alerts/

**HIS FOREVER** - An Alpha Billionaire Romance Serial
(Completed)


**RICHES TO RAGS** - A Stepbrother Romance
(Completed)


**NOT LOOKING FOR LOVE** - An NA Contemporary
Romance Series (Completed)

## ABOUT THE AUTHOR

Lena Bourne is a USA Today Bestselling contemporary romance author. She writes about alpha bad boys with a sensitive side and the alpha females who prove to be their match. Hot bedroom scenes and fast-paced, action packed plots are Lena's specialty. She's still waiting for her own HEA with the right bad boy, but the searching is lots of fun too. Coffee lover, owner of cats.

Sign up for Lena's newsletter to receive exclusive sneak peaks at new books, special mailing-list-only offers and other goodies. Copy and paste this link to join: http://www.lenabourne.com/the-list/

Connect with Lena online:

Facebook:
https://www.facebook.com/lenabourneauthor

Website: www.lenabourne.com
Twitter: https://twitter.com/Lena_Bourne

Made in the USA
Lexington, KY
29 August 2019